ACKNOWLE ....ENTS

My heartfelt thanks to family, friends, and the readers of my first novel *BIRDS ON A WIRE*. You could not realize your influence upon me saying you were, "...waiting for a second book." Collectively you spurred me onward.

To those of you who were my guides and sources of information, providing constructive criticism, history lessons, and corrections (Wendell R. Kay, Florence Singley Simmons, Ed Martin, Donna Dewey Kammer, Herb Strunk, Kathy Paul Rackley, Richard Winkler, Cindy Furman, Michael Lehutsky, and Jane Bailey D'Amore), thanks for setting me right. Even the most miniscule of contributions are important to me.

My love and thanks to Arthur, the family basset who for a decade altered the dynamics of our home. Forever will his arrival in our lives be a mystery. Artie is the hound I picture in this story, a true inspiration.

To Mr. Richard Teeter and Mr. John Karpiak, I have but one request:

Do not *ever again* take any book of mine into a BARNES & NOBLE. I still wake up hearing sirens.

In keeping with tradition: Hi, Mac! Hi, Rupe!

RABBIT TRAILS

WILL WYCKOFF

NADINE!

MY PLEASURE TO
MEET you & TRAVEL
DOWN MEMORY LANE!

Will

Copyright © 2015 Will Wyckoff

All Rights Reserved 3rd Edition

ISBN: 1511813652

ISBN 13: 9781511813655

Library of Congress Control Number: 2015906854

CreateSpace Independent Publishing Platform,

North Charleston, South Carolina

To Kay,
who tolerates my disappearances
into the Recluse Room

PROLOGUE

As a young adult looking back, it appears to me that most people who knew my grandfather liked him. He lived in Wayne County all his life, and there are moments when it seems that he crossed the paths of most of its inhabitants. Almost every county native I have met who is in his seventies seems to recall some sort of story about Jacob McGee, and all the stories make me proud. I am his grandson, and my name, too, is Jake McGee.

I love the man, and I miss him still. Therein lies the story. Family and friends still miss him, but they think he is gone—as in *dead*. Back when he disappeared, I was a seven year old, and of course, I wanted him found. Discovering him consumed me, and although my parents did not know it, I continued looking for him years later. At the very least, I wanted answers. After my many journeys made in an attempt to learn all I could, herein lies my discovery regarding my grandfather's disappearance.

CHAPTER 1

My grandfather was a salesman. A big man with a full head of thick, white hair, he was comparable to a giant teddy bear. He was fun to hug, fun to hold, and fun to have at my side. I would tell him things a little boy tells his grandfather but would never tell his parents. For example, my folks were pushing 4H on me, and when I shared with him how I did not want to join 4H, he kept it to himself.

"I want to learn that stuff from you, Gramps," I told him one day when we were out walking. "I don't want to go to meetings."

He replied, "Little Jake, you should try it. Give it a chance. It's all about things you and I enjoy." Secretly I think he agreed with Mom and Dad. All that being said, from what I could tell he had a big heart and gentle way about him most of the time. I think that's why he didn't take sides. Teddy bears don't do that.

Just looking at him I could tell he was a decent athlete at one time. I remember his large, strong hands, too. His grip was impressive. I mentioned it to him once. He taught me that no one gets to make a first impression twice, so a good handshake was important. "I think it sends a good message about your self-confidence," he told me. "A handshake suggests you have some control over your life." That was a lot for a seven year old to consider, yet I remember vividly right where I was when he said it. We were atop a fallen tree trunk as he was helping me cross a stream in the woods on his property.

For a living, my grandfather sold all sorts of beverages to all sorts of establishments: restaurants, taverns, county fair vendors, and even vendors in stadiums. Since he was successful and well-liked, he was not only assigned the largest sales region, but also a company car. In fact, no other salesman for Dougherty's Beverages was granted such a vehicle. Others were paid by the mile and given a stipend for using their own cars. Despite the company perk, he was respected by his co-workers. They knew he was offered a salary while they worked on commissions. To no surprise to those who knew him, my gramps chose to work on commission as well. My dad once told me that Grampa thought it was better for everyone that he not be treated differently regarding his paycheck, and that being on commission helped him keep his competitive edge.

Toward the end of his career, Grampa was honored by our local papers. *The News Eagle*, *The Independent*, and *The River Reporter* each reported how he had driven over a million miles while on the job but was never in an accident. However when friends were around, my dad used to tease Grampa and say to him, "But they never reported how many accidents you caused!" Dad could say such things to his father because, as

Grampa used to say to me, "McGees have a thick skin and a good sense of humor."

When he was not on the road, Grampa loved two things above all else: family and the outdoors. His love of the woods was immeasurable. He knew all the species of birds and their calls. Forest animals benefited from Grampa's interest in them, for he often fed those who did not hibernate. Throughout the winter months, my father, my grandfather and I dropped off bales of straw and bags of feed from the back of our pickup truck. Critters in the field were provided cover when we piled any cut brush where they could hide. Field animals were provided food as well. All of it was strategically served in the middle of unused culvert pipes located above ground for easy access and where their feed kept dry from the weather. A mixture of corn, grains, and molasses, it was transported in burlap bags for placement in those lengthy, metal pipes across his property beyond my grandparents' home. As the animals fed, we used binoculars and enjoyed watching them visit on a regular basis.

In warmer weather, many were the weekends when the five of us would camp overnight or have a Saturday picnic together. Gramma McGee and Mom would prep our picnic baskets with delicious surprises, while Grampa, Dad, and I would march through the woods or go fishing in a pond on the family property. We would even take Grampa's basset Artie with us.

"I wonder where this young pup will lead us today," he would always say when he turned Artie loose in the back field. "For their own safety, rabbits run in so many directions.

3

I have often wondered how he makes up his mind about which trail to follow."

"The most recent scent is probably the strongest," I recall my dad saying to both of us. That made sense to a little boy.

My mother's parents were always invited, too, and sometimes they would join us for a good time. My mom was an Ashton. Her parents, Bill and Nancy Ashton, were always generous regarding what they would bring to our outings. It was not at all unusual for us to find ourselves returning to the house with tons of leftover food.

Sadly, such outings ended on June 28th of 2009 when my grandfather disappeared. Just disappeared. My grandmother Ginny Gale McGee told us that it was not uncommon for Grampa to call out that he was "…going for a walk. I'll be back later!" He always took an ample supply of water and was fond of carrying a walking stick, a gnarly old tree branch he varnished long ago.

"Just be careful!" she told us she sang out to him that day, and he hiked off happily into an environment he loved.

When questioned, she told officials that she never suspected that he would be gone for good. She was certain he felt well. It was not a day rife with ominous signs. There were no storms. Weather on that Sunday was sunny, and it was not at all humid. He just did not come home. She told us she had begun to worry, so she finally called us around dinner time. We left our plates right on our kitchen table as we locked up and headed to their house, hoping he would have returned by the time we arrived.

CHAPTER 2

At summer vacation's end, I was to enter second grade assigned to Mrs. Keen's class. Mom somehow had ways of learning such things as class assignments ahead of time. I was comfortable with her as a teacher for Mrs. Keen had been a friend of the family for quite some time. In fact, her father Mr. Corey had put the roof on Grampa's house. So it was not a big surprise to anyone but me when Mrs. Keen and her parents showed up at Grampa's house to help comfort Gramma and to search for my missing grandfather as well.

That was how I learned who would be my teacher in the fall, and I know I will never forget my first impression. She had a soft voice and a pretty smile. I remember, too, that she was really tan and had straight, dark hair to her shoulders. She was not very tall, or so it seemed to me, but immediately I liked her. My decision to like her was not based upon her appearance. I was impressed by the fact that she was there to help. To me, that spoke volumes about the Corey clan. If I did not learn anything else that Sunday in June, I learned that real family friends show up when it matters the most.

Gramps told a story once about the power of friends and community involvement. A local Waymart family lost their barn, and to them it was a major blow to their farming operation. Their barn happened to be of enormous proportions, more than a place to park family cars, snow blowers and lawn mowers. They needed it not only for storing their equipment and tools, but also to house and care for their livestock. He told us how on an appointed day not too long after the blaze, volunteers arrived at the family's home in great numbers to share their various talents. I was amazed to learn how a community could come together like that and, as Grampa told it, "..put a deserving family back on its feet."

Perhaps that is why, in part, the McGee place was quickly swamped with search and rescue volunteers. Hundreds heeded our call for help, and I remember thinking how during my entire life I had never seen so many flashing lights in one place. The driveway was packed all the way out to the main road with all sorts of emergency vehicles, fire trucks, and police cars. Some were red, some were yellow, and the rest were the common colors of everyday vehicles, but all of them had flashing lights.

An efficient organizational meeting outside of my grandparents' house started things off. I could hear excited, muffled voices all about. My seven year old brain found it obvious that they were eager to begin, but they waited respectfully for their orders. Two or three men stood at the end of the veranda so they could be heard assigning areas or "grids" to be searched. Also, the organizers' assistants took roll while emphasizing to everyone that when the recovery efforts were completed they were to be certain to sign out at the headquarters-like station that had quickly been set up on the porch. It was clear they were optimistic.

"It's very important that we be organized!" one officer shouted. "We do not want to leave any volunteers out in the woods who might be injured and unaccounted for." Then he added a scary thought. "We don't want to have to set up a search party for a volunteer."

I was the only child among the adults on that big, old wrap-around porch at the moment. "Hopefully this won't take long," are the five words I will never forget Mr. Pratt uttering to no one in particular. I was standing next to him when he said it. He was the Fire Chief, and I was sure hoping the same thing. A tall, thin physically fit man, he saw me and placed his arm around my shoulders. I had met him once or twice before at our school when he visited during Fire Prevention Week each October. He ran a program to help kids look for dangers around their homes. Chief Pratt's face was kind, and I was sure he would take care of everything when he said to me, "We're on our way, Little Jake."

As quickly as all those folks assembled, they dispersed into the woods and down the road, receding from our property like a wave returning to its ocean. There one moment and gone the next. That left a skeleton crew which remained behind sitting on the porch, serving as the Base of Operations or Headquarters.

I remember two sounds vividly from that Sunday afternoon after the search had begun. The first is the static-filled sound of their hand-held radios, and the other is my grandmother's sobbing. She kept telling us how she would miss her husband, but had to keep the faith, that they *would* be reunited.

Gramma was Grampa's prize. Around their house, various pictures of my grandparents depicted them at various stages in their life together as a happy, good-looking couple. My dad was a little guy for a while, but not for long as the family photos revealed.

For their first anniversary, my grandfather surprised her with a golden, heart-shaped locket. Dad said that for as long as he could recall she wore it every single day, and it was not until I was in first grade that I learned there was a photo inside of it. A photographer had captured the moment Gramma and her groom stood beside their first car ready to depart for their honeymoon. It was then that I saw her for the first time as a younger woman, and even as a boy I realized she was stunning.

Grampa bragged how Codger Menke and many others tried to win her affection, but he was the one who "... got under her skin and into her heart." It hurt us terribly to listen to her crying.

Only a week after the summer solstice, daylight lingered and afforded searchers more valuable time. As reports came back to the base, and grids were checked off as having been thoroughly searched, and new quadrants were assigned to the crews, I was able to look on their map and watch the calculated search take place. For a while, envisioning the search was a help to me, but after a couple of hours I started to worry more when I realized just how vast an area there was to be searched. I had been out there and had experienced it first-hand, and I knew what they were attempting was no easy task.

I took Mom aside when I could and asked, "Mom, are they going to find Grampa?"

She did her best to assure me when she whispered, "There are many, many folks helping search, Jake." But I also heard what she was *not* saying: "They will find him." That first day I was not permitted to search with anyone else, and I remember that frustrated me to no end.

My grandfather had a term for what I had become. The term was "blivvy", and as he explained it, "That's when you have ten pounds of energy in a two-pound bottle!" He said blivvies were what made kids anxious. I felt as if I was about to explode that two-pound bottle into a million pieces.

CHAPTER 3

Darkness settled over our property like a thick blanket I wished I could shed. I was sitting on their porch glider next to Gramma. Despite her broken heart, she insisted on being there to thank as many participants as possible as they returned from their search. The floating voices of these tired men and women were almost ghostly. I heard them, but I did not see them. What I noticed most of all was the disappointment each expressed without even speaking of it. To my ear, the tones of their respective voices were almost apologetic. I felt bad for them.

One gentleman's soft voice shared how there were moments during his search when he experienced a sense of communications or messages. "It was eerie. I began wondering if I was subjected to divine intervention."

To his comment only silence answered him. No one commented upon his report.

"I guess I'm just tired," was how he passed it off. He drifted away with the others toward their vehicles, nothing more than silhouettes.

That moment and that man's comment stuck with me. It was nearly dark when he said it. What I remember most about hearing those softly spoken words is Gramma's reaction. She gasped quietly. She made no comment, but she definitely gasped. It was as if that particular volunteer had struck a chord with her. Later we learned he was the pastor of a church thirty miles north of us.

People tried so hard to find my grandfather, but had come up empty-handed. Occasionally I heard volunteers say something like, "Maybe tomorrow we'll have better luck," but that tomorrow of which they spoke never came.

They returned for days. Some were new to the mix, and their fresh determination invigorated others who were perhaps losing hope. "Today's the day. I can feel it," were the words of one young woman. My hopes rode on her shoulders. But no one ever found my grampa. No one. Eventually a day came when my dad agreed to something I never thought he would: terminating the search. That was when I cried the most. We all did.

Summer turned to fall, and I was in school. Mrs. Keen proved to be even nicer than I imagined possible. She was the first person other than my parents who took me for walks in the woods. I never told her I went with her looking for my grandfather, but she knew what I was doing. We would talk about anything at all. Nothing was considered off-limits.

"Jake," she said one day, "it's okay to keep up your hopes."

I was shocked when she said it. No one told me it was okay.

Until that moment right there by her side in the woods, I felt like I was silently being molded into the mindset that everyone else seemed to have accepted: "Grampa was not coming back. There was nothing more to be done." I understood that, but I did not really accept it. I needed answers. The one question I needed answered most of all was, "Why can't he still be alive someplace?" Mrs. Keen was the first person I ever asked.

I remember it like it was yesterday. She stopped walking, and she tugged at my arm. "Jake, what are you thinking? You haven't spoken a word in twenty minutes." We were both wearing jeans, and both of us wore hooded sweatshirts that day. It was a chilly and grand day in autumn; the stuff of post cards and paintings people place over a mantel.

She had long ago won my confidence, so I just spoke my answer straight out. "Why can't my grandfather still be alive someplace?"

She gently pulled her burgundy hood from her head as if she wanted to hear me better, but then I realized that was not the case when gently she said to me, "*Maybe he is.*"

Those three words changed a lot for me. Did she realize she was giving me hope? Was my second grade teacher *slash* family friend giving me hope? I was stunned. I was unprepared for her reply. No one had given me hope since the search was terminated more than two months earlier.

"Mrs. Keen, you don't think it's wrong that I hope and wish he's still alive?"

"No, Jake, but it might be best if we keep this kind of thinking between us for now."

I knew what she was saying. She did not want anyone else thinking we were crazy.

"This can be our little secret, although it's not little when it comes to importance." She went on to tell me that she would like me to report back to her just how things were going. She understood that in my own way I would continue my search for Grampa, but she wanted me to check in with her from time to time and provide her with my updates.

Before that day, my school year was nice. After that day, second grade was amazing. Mrs. Keen taught the class little things like mapping and even some survival skills. For example, she taught us about lighting a campfire with a lens.

One day, during science class, from her desk she pulled out a nine-volt battery and pad of steel wood. She sent me to the boys' lavatory for a few sheets of toilet paper. Upon my return, she had us stand in a semi-circle around a table where she sat. When we quieted she began her lesson.

"What happens to your fingers when you touch both posts of this battery at the same time?" She looked at our curious faces. "Anybody want to guess?" Still no takers.

"Okay, does anyone know what batteries store inside of them?"

In various ways, more than a few of us replied how electricity was stored for flashlights, smoke alarms, and remote controls.

"Ok then, what is electricity? How do we use it? Why would we want to store it?"

More answers. From our answers, of course, she learned what we knew, and that led to other things. She talked briefly about how wires or metal contacts were needed to be the "...

highways for the electricity..." to travel from one place to another.

"Okay," she said, "before I show you something neat, I want to teach you one of the ways that electricity can be dangerous." We were silent.

Tearing a three-inch piece of steel wool from its pad, she twisted it into a wire-like shape. We moved closer.

"Now watch what happens when I touch this steel wool to one of the posts." We waited. We watched. Nothing happened.

"Well? What happened?" she inquired of our group of scientists.

"Nothing," we said rather disappointed.

"Uh huh. That's right." Then she made her voice sound mysterious when she added, "But watch what happens now when I touch the other end to the second post."

"Wow!" was the response of everyone when we saw the steel wool instantly glow orange and melt into little, charred pieces.

She went on to explain why the metal wire turned orange. Heat, a lot of heat, was the result of the electricity traveling along its highway of steel wool.

"Now we will do this one more time, kids, but this time we'll let the glowing wire touch the toilet paper." She asked us to make predictions concerning what we thought would happen. Seeing the paper burst into flame was incredible. The rest of the lesson we talked about how this experiment might be useful.

At discussion's end, she looked directly at me and said, "If we had enough dry, thin grass we could even start a campfire." I never forgot that day.

During reading class, she sometimes picked adventure stories and rescue stories for us to read aloud together. My classmates and I would discuss them, and from those stories I learned a lot. She did it for everyone, but I think most of all she was doing it for me. I kept searching.

CHAPTER 4

Richard "Codger" Menke grew up in Wayne County, named for Anthony Wayne, statesman and once General in Chief of the Army during the Revolutionary War. If locals were surveyed over a cup of coffee in any of the county's eateries, most folks would describe the area as largely rural. Too, they would probably be quick to point out its significant historical markers.

Hailed as The Birthplace of the American Railroad, Honesdale's business roots grabbed hold in the early 1800's when anthracite coal was discovered in abundance not far away. The need to transport the fuel to New York City brought about many business opportunities including the Delaware and Hudson Canal Company and later the railroading industry.

Business was booming throughout the nineteenth century, and some would say that the Menkes were in it up to their knees. Two hundred years later, a keen interest in making a buck still ran through Richard Menke's blood. Some would say he was obsessed.

Codger was elected a Wayne County Commissioner in 1996, and he quickly built a reputation as a shrewd individual, not necessarily well-liked. Like others before him, he made campaign promises and not only failed to keep them, but forgot all about them once he was in office.

The word around the county was that he was the deciding vote on a controversial quarry project. Commissioner Menke knew full well the fate of an entire mountain full of trees and forest animals, not to mention the people who called the area home, rested on his vote. Legend has it that his position on the issue went from environmentalist to progressive as fast as the new truck he began driving not long after the quarry opened.

The original Wayne County Courthouse opened in 1884, but the offices of each modern day commissioner were established at the back side of the Courthouse Annex which was completed in 1972. These offices overlooked the Lackawaxen River which eventually flows into the Delaware. Codger Menke's office was the largest of the three.

"Mr. Menke? Mr. Menke?" His secretary waited for him to answer. She was accustomed to prolonged waits. Codger Menke liked being a County Commissioner, but he liked it on his own terms. He did not like to take calls. Too often they meant making promises to constituents, promises he would never keep. Often those calls meant more meetings, or they meant just plain work. "Mr. Menke?"

Finally he acknowledged. "Yes, Margaret."

"Mr. Menke, you have a call from Crown Developers. May I put it through to you?"

Up went his eyebrows. This call had the potential to put money in his pocket. Richard "Codger" Menke liked this kind of call. It was the reason he wanted to be Commissioner in the first place.

"Sure! I'd like to talk to them, Margaret. Put their call through to me." He waited just a moment, collected his thoughts and said, "Hello?"

"Mr. Richard Menke?"

"Yes, speaking!" Codger used his *Let's see what this sucker wants* voice. "How may I help you?"

The gentleman on the other end of the call was David Crown, the owner and President of Crown Developers. His name was not unknown throughout the area. In fact, when the Courthouse Annex was constructed, it was David Crown's family who won the contract. To the original courthouse, expansion dictated that a five-floor office building be attached, and it was done in such a way that the grand old building's original brick architecture was never compromised. From the basement, where the Engineering, Maintenance, and Purchasing Departments were placed, to the top floor offices of various officials, the work was beautifully done, all by Crown Developers.

"Dave Crown here, Mr. Menke. We've never spoken before. I wanted to touch bases with you regarding the construction of the Catskills Spur off of the Casey Highway near Carbondale." Mr. Crown's voice was business-like, but he was pleasant. "We plan to bid on that highway project, and I want to make sure we are jumping through all the correct hoops to have a chance to land the project."

"Nice of you to call," replied the wily, greedy commissioner. He knew he had something worth considering and something the President of Crown Developers wanted. "Usually I deal with minions."

"You won't have that problem here, Mr. Menke. You'll deal only with me if it suits you."

"I'd like that," thought Codger sarcastically to himself. What he really wanted to say is that he would like it as long as it was not too big of a nuisance.

"I have to ask you, Mr. Crown. Has the Department of Conservation's Real Estate Division finalized which particular stretch of land will be developed?" Secretly Codger was hoping it might be a piece he owned, providing yet another opportunity to line his pockets.

"No, Sir. I don't have the specifics yet. That's why I'm calling you." He went on to speak of how the Pennsylvania Department of Transportation was able to get legislation passed, thereby making the new highway construction possible. "I am trying to get a feel for how large of an undertaking this will be. I'd like to bid competitively, not be way off target."

"Well, Mr. Crown–"

"Mr. Menke, call me Dave."

"Well, Dave, it will run all the way from Carbondale's Route 6 to Livingston Manor's Route 17. It's quite lengthy, and I can tell you it won't be too popular with the locals." He thought a bit. "I guess it's about thirty-five to forty miles over pretty rural land, and as I think you might already suspect, some if it might run through State Game Lands."

"Okay. That's a start. I appreciate the info." Crown was smart enough not to reveal just how much he did know.

Codger was doing the math in his head while Mr. Crown spoke. He quickly understood this was easily a $50,000,000 project. No wonder Mr. Crown was interested. Codger was more than interested. He was excited at the prospect of improving his own financial situation, too. He thought about this so long that Mr. Crown was not sure Menke was still on the phone.

"Mr. Menke? Are you still there?"

"Yes." He cleared his throat. "Excuse me, Dave. Let me get back to you, and I'll see if I can grease the wheels for you, so to speak. No promises, of course, but you know the old saying, 'If you scratch my back, I'll scratch yours'."

Mr. Crown knew *exactly* what Richard "Codger" Menke was saying...and not saying. Initially Mr. Crown wondered whether or not he had contacted the right commissioner. He had indeed.

"Okay, Mr. Menke. I'm glad I called. I look forward to doing business with you and, of course, the other commissioners as well. Have a good one."

It took but seconds to hang up his phone, come from behind his oak desk, and quietly close his office door. Codger Menke walked over to the office maps of Wayne County and neighboring Lackawanna County. As he stood before them, he studied the land from Carbondale to Livingston Manor. In his most sly and diabolical voice he whispered to himself, "Well well well, Mr. Jacob McGee, my old foe, at long last I'm finally going to get some revenge."

As far back as he cared to recall, it seemed to Richard Menke that Jacob McGee had always beaten him to any opportunity. "I don't know why you disappeared, and it doesn't matter to me. It will just feel good to make your family squirm."

CHAPTER 5

Through the beginning of August, I felt that my summer prior to eighth grade would not be anything to brag about when writing the traditional September composition regarding summer vacation. We all knew it would be assigned in class, and I had nothing. I enjoyed time away from school, but I had to admit I missed my school buddies. Most of them lived in town. I even missed the school bullies since they, at least, added some excitement to our school day. By the end of July, vacation was hot, humid, and almost boring.

The son of a carpenter, I lived with my parents and my grandmother on what was once my paternal grandparents' property among the hills of Northeastern Pennsylvania ten miles outside of Honesdale. Dan McGee, my dad, grew up on this same tract of land, a seven-acre parcel which was bordered by State Game Lands. My grandfather picked up the property in the 1975, "...for a mere bag of shells..." as he was fond of saying. At the time, he was only twenty-five, but he knew a good value when he saw one. Just out of the navy and married only a few years, he borrowed enough money from the bank to seal the deal. There were others who wanted to do the same, but he acted first and made one or two people jealous, especially Richard "Codger" Menke, the only person Grampa did not trust.

My grandfather told me about a time when he was a teen and how Codger had his eye on Gramma. Suffice it to say that did not go well for Grampa's rival either.

"Ol' Codger even resorted to spreading some not-so-nice rumors," my grandfather once told me over an iced tea on his porch. "He tried to blame some pollution woes down the road on a garbage dump I established way out back."

"You have a dump, Gramps?"

"No, Little Jake," he chuckled. "That's the point. He said our stream passed through my dump and poisoned the run off. I don't even have a dump. Never did! What a waste of the inspector's time that was, trying to find a dump that never existed."

Along with a small pond, there was a rocky stream that snaked and nestled among the groves of maples and evergreens before it disappeared into the game land woods. During the summer before eighth grade, our homestead was all that stood between complete boredom and myself. At least I had my exploring, something Mrs. Keen said years earlier was okay to do.

When I explored the woods, I often thought of my grandfather. I never lost sight of the fact that he was my reason I explored so frequently. He was an avid outdoorsman, well-respected in the community, and a great deal of fun. Whenever

I think back about it, I recall how I had always enjoyed our hikes in the woods together.

Wherever I traveled locally, it seemed that someone had a story to share about my grampa, Jacob McGee. More than once I heard about a day in January of 1982 when my grandfather single-handedly subdued a pair of bank robbers outside one of our local banks.

"Son, your grandfather stopped those two thugs right at the opening curtain of their performance," the local grocer Mr. Jenkins told me as he bagged for my mom. I stood respectfully quiet as folks walked by and offered a look of curiosity.

"He was a sharp fella, your grandfather. Through the Dime Bank's drive-in window, your gramps quickly sized up what was taking place inside the bank. She was young back then, but it was Melissa Gardepe's frightened face in the window that tipped him off."

Mr. Jenkins kept bagging as he spoke. "Jacob quickly circled the bank parking lot and waited for those two hoodlums to exit."

At this point in the often-told tale, I felt compelled to play my part by speaking up and asking, "What did my grampa do next, Mr. Jenkins?" even though I knew the story well. My interest was always keen, and this grandson never tired of hearing the story. Finished with her shopping, even my mom would stand by and let it all be told again as well. It was always at this point in the story that neither of us knew which ending would be revisited or if a new one was about to be hatched!

"Jake," Mr. Jenkins said excitedly, "I'll tell ya. Your grandfather decided right then and there that his big red Power Wagon with its yellow plow blade was his weapon of choice." By now, Mr. Jenkins had stopped everything he was doing.

"No sooner did those crooks hop into their little foreign getaway car, than your grandfather made them part of the bank's exterior! They were pinned there until the police arrived shortly afterward to finish the job."

There *was* one constant whenever the story was told. I always took pride in asking one last question. "Why do you think he did it?"

"Jake, my boy, somebody asked your grandfather that very question after all was said and done. I want you to know he refused to be labeled a hero, and he simply told everyone he met that he'd worked too darned hard for his money to let somebody steal it."

No matter how many times our family heard that tale about young Jacob McGee back in the 80's, the fella with a pretty wife and young son, the one who stopped the bank robbery, we enjoyed the story and felt a surge of family pride. Nor did it matter one bit what version we were hearing.

With time on my hands, I enjoyed such memories while I explored. To prevent jumping out of my skin, many summer days were filled with exploration for hours on end. I made a few discoveries on my own that summer. There was the occasional skull of a deer or a coon, of course, and I have never forgotten the first time I found antlers that had been shed. It was not an easy find. Perhaps my favorite discoveries were bits of obsolete technology like a well house or cold spring shaped out of fieldstone. Terrific water still ran through them.

Perhaps the most creepy discovery occurred the day I hiked into a clearing over which deer hair was strewn across an area roughly fifty feet in diameter. Not at all unlike the results of a giant pillow fight when feathers are cast about, the deer hair was all over weeds, branches, bushes and rocks, yet I found no carcass. When I told my dad later that day, he gave me the chills when he said I had come across a location where a pack of coyotes had captured a deer, and in a frenzy they killed it.

"You found no carcass because they eventually dragged it away." He thought it was good Artie was not with me that day, for our basset might have followed their trail.

I inherited Artie from Grampa, and following him was always an adventure. The forest provided an abundance of small game, hiding places, and trails we two had never traversed. My family's land, along with the game land acreage bordering it, was paradise to this tri-colored chunk of muscle. Unleashed when there was no hunting season, my four-legged friend disappeared quickly. His occasional howls sounded through the trees and revealed his location to my trained ear, and I enjoyed following in pursuit. It was during these days Artie would shed his lazy, lie-around-the-house personality, and he adopted a nearly reckless, ears-back, full-speed-ahead attitude towards hunting and sniffing.

Once when I was ten and in the fifth grade, we set out on our first journey together into the woods on the back of our property. It was proved to be both frightening and educational.

Until that day, I had no previous experience taking him by myself, and I was upset when Artie left my side seemingly forever. The hound sang his song from time to time, but to me it was a song about *goodbye*.

I just could not keep up with the pace Artie set as he scouted up and down the hills throughout those woods thick with mountain laurel, pines, and maples. After hours of walking and calling to my hound, I finally returned home late in the afternoon worried about my dog's safety. I was dubious as to whether or not I would ever see him again, and I felt awful that I had somehow let my grandfather down.

Upon arriving home, Dad commented upon my downhearted expression. "You don't look so good, Sport. What's wrong?" My father was a powerfully built man, about six feet tall, with thick, brown hair, and calloused hands he earned through his trade. But he was every bit as caring and loving as he was tough.

Dad had been reading a magazine on the spindled veranda outside the kitchen. The railing and porch floor he repaired all by himself decorated our old homestead three-fourths the way around. When I found him he was sitting in the shade on the glider, and I began explaining my dilemma to him while he listened.

Upset with myself, the situation I was in, and nearly in tears, I explained the empty leash in my hand. Dad calmly asked me to sit by his side, and he listened. Then he offered me some advice.

"First of all, before your grandfather vanished, he used to take Artie in the woods. That was long before he took you." Then my dad added, "And I used to have a basset I called Corky. I've told you about her. She was brown, black, and white, too."

Then he continued. "When I'd let her run, she was just like Artie. Probably all bassets are. She roamed the woods around here 'til eventually she decided it was time to return. I couldn't always keep up, nor could I make her follow me home when I was ready to come home."

I looked up at my father and asked in a worried-but-hopeful voice, "What did you do to get her back?"

"I took off my shirt–."

"What?" I interrupted suddenly as if not ready to believe my own father. For a second, I wondered if he was just busting on me.

Dad continued, "Let me finish! I would take off my shirt or sweatshirt and lay it on the ground right where I had released her. Eventually she returned to that very same place, found my shirt or sweatshirt, and she waited for me in that location." He went on to explain how bassets, beagles, and other hounds circle because rabbits and other animals always run away from their nests. "Then they eventually return as well. The dog follows their scented trail, and thus the cycle is completed."

Almost before Dad could finish, I was off and running to the woods while trying to remove my shirt as I ran. Later he told me that I nearly ran smack into the oak tree by the back fence when my shirt became tangled over my head! It was not long after that when I discovered Artie ambling calmly across our back field. His head was down as he was sniffing. He did not seem to have a care in the world, and I was never so happy to see him. On that day, I had no reason to leave my shirt behind. However, there were other afternoons when that piece of sage advice turned out to be just what the doctor ordered. Three years passed.

CHAPTER 6

My mother dried her hands and picked up the phone. As she balanced it between her ear and her shoulder she spoke, continuing to put away groceries. Through the window over our kitchen sink, she spotted Netty Carter coming up our gravel driveway, her long brown hair in braids. Since I was upstairs in my room, Mom called to me regarding Netty's arrival, apologized to her friend on the phone, and continued listening.

Netty Carter was my best friend and a classmate. She lived just down the road and had been in my class since the fifth grade when Mr. McElroy was our teacher. Besides numbers and new words, Mr. "Mac" taught me a most important lesson: some girls can be pretty cool. Netty was one of them. Until fifth grade, boys just did *not* play with girls. It was a universal law or something. However, little by little, and after the normal amount of teasing, Netty began to fit into my day better than most of the boys in my age group.

Our friendship began one bright Tuesday during recess, as other kids scooted around our playground like water bugs on the nearby pond. I asked Alonzo Preen to help me catch some bugs for science class. "Come on, 'Zo! I bet Mr. Mac will give us some extra credit!"

Alonzo balked at the concept of touching bugs and jogged off to a game of dodge ball. Seconds later I heard Netty quietly say, "I bet I can catch more than you can." I looked up and was surprised to find the challenge had been issued by my neighbor. A girl! She was the girl from down our road, and she had the longest hair I had ever seen. Together we caught several creatures that we found under rocks and among some thick bushes which defined the playground. On that day, Netty actually caught the most. Mr. Mac was indeed quite pleased and added our catch to the classroom's terrarium and display boxes. Even Alonzo was impressed.

"It was Jake's idea," I heard Netty say to Mr. Mac, "and we had fun catching them." My opinion of Netty changed a lot on that Tuesday. My teacher was right. The foundation for our friendship had been poured, and we have been friends ever since.

As it turned out, I learned a lot about collecting insects from Netty Carter. She even had her own collection at home. She taught me all sorts of things. For example, we used different kinds of nets. I thought a net was just a net.

"This is a butterfly net," she said to me one day before we went out on a hunt. "It is made from a lightweight mesh so we don't damage delicate butterfly wings." Then she picked up another net which had a shorter handle. "This is a sweep net. It is used to collect insects from grass and taller brush." She compared the two in front of me. "It is similar to a butterfly net, except that its bag is made from tougher material because it is whipped back and forth through taller grasses which would rip a butterfly net."

I looked at her amazed that any kid could know so much about insects. Finally I just said, "Show me your collection." I followed her, a peanut of a girl at that time, into her garage where her parents let her keep it. She had seven display boxes neatly arranged on part of the wall in the back. She showed me all sorts of insects including bees, ants, crickets, moths, and butterflies of different colors.

As we looked at all seven boxes, she said to me quietly, "Did you know there's even an assassin bug?"

"Really? Cool. Do you have one of them?"

"No. It's a goal of mine to get one someday." She went on to teach me what makes an insect an insect. "They have to have three body parts: the head, the thorax, and an abdomen. I recognize them, but don't ask me what the last two are for." We both laughed after she said it.

"What else?" I could tell she was enjoying the moment.

"Believe it or not, they each have to have three pairs of jointed legs, one pair of antennae, and something called compound eyes." She looked at me, and I noticed her long hair was tossed by the wind, some of it caught in the corners of her mouth. I have never forgotten that day.

Despite my teacher's advice about girls, I did take some heat from some of the guys in our grade at school. In particular, Jeremy Teller was a thorn in my side. He teased Netty and me unmercifully while bullying other guys in our class to do the same. Jeremy was so much larger than the rest of us that he could intimidate others into saying or doing things they ordinarily would not. It was not at all unusual for him to get into trouble at school, but being made to eat alone during lunch did not seem to bother him.

"Hey, Everyone! Look! There goes Jake and his girl-friend, Fishnetty!" Or whenever we were together at recess he would summon his loudest voice and yell across the school-yard, "When's the wedding?"

As best we could, we would ignore him, and we tried to appear as if everyone's nervous laughter did not bother us, but it did. Two things in particular bothered me. First of all, once in a while he could bully some of my friends into laughing at us. I understood that he was big and scary, but I never would have sided against them because of him. That really hurt.

Most of all, what *really* annoyed me was that he was Mr. Menke's grandson, and Mr. Menke was *the one guy* my grand-father did not like or trust. Sometimes I wondered if Jeremy Teller's grandfather coached Jeremy or instructed him to be mean to me. I wondered if he knew I was Jake McGee's grandson. How could he not? Gramps and I shared the same name.

For a time, I ignored him as my parents had suggested, but there finally came the day when I was tired of his unchecked rants. It was Picture Day at school, and even Jeremy wore nicer-than-usual clothes to school, so I came up with a plan.

Our cafeteria was always loud, and even though we were supposed to remain seated while we ate, most of us were antsy and figured out ways to gain permission to move about the caf-eteria. We would raise our hands and ask to go to the lavatory, or we would just hop up and go grab a spoon we pretended to forget the first time through the lunch line. When we were *really* desperate, we would pretend we wanted a second helping of school food, but no one believed *that* was true. My plan sort of fell into that category.

I cannot imagine what a lunch room would be like in any school if not for the presence of teachers and lunch workers. It was zoo-like in our school, so some things just were not noticed. I hoped that my rising and walking to the lunch lady at the cash register seemed rather ordinary. My purchase of extra tomato soup and a second grilled cheese had been performed by countless others. But that day when I accidentally spilled all my soup on Jeremy Teller's white shirt, the chance of going unnoticed was the last thing on my mind. I wanted everyone to see what happened, and that it was me who caused the commotion.

That was another cool thing about Mr. McElroy. He seemed to have his finger on the pulse of the school. No sooner had I pretended to stumble and spilled the soup all over my nemesis's shoulder and his back, Mr. McElroy was right on top of things and kept me from being annihilated. I never asked him, but I have long since wondered how he knew what I was thinking. It might have been my very first experience with something he taught us in science: ESP or extra sensory perception! And yes, for a while, Teller left us alone.

Netty walked into my bedroom and said hello. Despite my mother's earlier announcement, we both knew Netty was always welcome to walk in anytime, so I had never left my room to meet her down at the door. However, on this occasion,

Gramma met her at the door, letting her in to see me. The arrangement was much the same at the Carter residence where I had become a regular fixture. She plopped upon my beanbag chair that hissed its customary, airy hiss upon her landing.

"Whatcha doin', Jake? What are we gonna do today?"

"You know what, Netty? Our vacation is nearly over, and we haven't found a new spot in the woods yet for our next outpost." I produced the crude map we began creating together weeks earlier, spreading it on my bed. On it were three triangles or "pyramids" as we labeled them. "Our first three stations are here, here, and here by the stream. We've stocked them with supplies, but we've never gone far into the woods."

By the use of various symbols and lines, our curled, parchment-colored paper took on the look of a pirate's treasure map from long ago. Groves of deciduous and coniferous trees were easily recognizable. The stream passing through the McGee family property was represented by a trio of wavy yet nearly-parallel lines. North, south, east and west were charted, albeit a little incorrectly, while the uneven terrain of the woods and meadows were a bit less understandable. Netty looked at me and uttered the five words that were indicative of our unselfish friendship: "It's your turn to lead."

CHAPTER 7

Whenever we searched for a site for a new outpost, Netty and I felt an increased energy. At the outset, we were not even in total agreement as to why we did such a thing, but both of us agreed it was fun. Other than confiding in Mrs. Keen years earlier, I kept my biggest reason for exploring the woods to myself, although I might have told my basset confidante Artie once a while back.

Outposts were locations that offered certain outdoorsy characteristics. If at all possible, being near water was a plus. However, it was preferred these spots be above nearby water levels to avoid unexpected flooding. Shade, too, was a priority. Netty preferred the shelter of evergreen trees like pine, hemlock, or tamarack because such trees had a pleasant fragrance and were seemingly cleaner at their trunks. She reasoned leafy or deciduous trees left decayed, moist leaves on the ground at their base.

Finally after a short snack of Mom's best cookies, we told my mother we were off on a hike, and that we would return in time for dinner. Netty, of course, was invited. She accepted the invitation, and requested my mother to tell her mother our plans. Mom agreed to do so saying, "I planned to call her today anyway. You two be careful. Are you taking Artie with you?"

"Not today, Mom," I replied as I snagged a final treat. "We don't have enough time to follow him today." I looked at Artie's sad, begging expression that is a famous characteristic of the basset breed. It bothered me a little to leave Artie at home whenever we left, but I felt today we would cover more new ground if we left him behind.

As two adventurers might, Netty and I set out excitedly across the back field of the our homestead's property. Stone walls, indigenous to northern farmlands established long ago, stood about waste high and separated the open fields into many sections. The gray walls were dotted with lichen and ivy, and some walls had begun to crumble under the force of many winters.

When hiking with my father once, he pointed to the walls and told me how he considered the construction of the local walls an incredible achievement. As I looked at all the stones individually for the first time, not the individual walls but the actual stones from which they were built, I gained a newfound respect regarding what men can do with the most ordinary tools: their hands, a strong back, good horses, a wagon, a shovel, and a pick.

Since our family was not farming these fields at all, new trees were sprouting here and there. Most were young maples. In fact, on an earlier expedition, Netty and I discovered a number of stone partitions in the woods beyond the more familiar fields. To us it was a mysterious find. From asking my dad about this, we learned that at one time many years ago the number of fields we now visited was even larger. He explained that we had merely stumbled upon some young trees where even more farm fields used to be.

On this particular August day, however, we had one thing in mind: discovering a deeper part of the game lands, sites upon which neither of us had set foot before. In the beginning of our trip that day, it was the sole reason we kept up a jogger's pace. Finally we reached the stream which divided "McGee" land and the game lands. To replenish our energy, we sat upon a mammoth rock we had enjoyed many times before. Sunlight through the trees spangled the huge, old boulder with shadows and beams of bright light.

"Okay, Jake. Which way are we headed?"

I was checking myself for ticks as I pondered Netty's question. Yet another thing I had learned from my dad was that it never hurt to be too cautious. To me, it made sense. Netty felt differently. She was "...catching some rays" while she awaited my decision. After a moment of thought, I spoke.

"Netty," I remember asking quietly and almost mysteriously, "how much have I told you about my grandfather?"

I was looking skyward but off to my side I could feel her looking at me. "Not much. I know he was gone before you and I became friends." Perhaps she sensed I was about to share something private; something special.

"Gone," I sort of laughed to myself as I repeated her choice of word. "It's odd that you would say 'gone' instead of 'dead' or 'deceased'."

"What?" she asked quizzically.

I still avoided eye contact. I busied myself by whipping stones into the shallow stream nearby. After pausing again, I spoke. "Netty, my grandfather is gone, but he might not be dead. I'm hoping I can find him alive."

CHAPTER 8

Jake's dad looked over the top of his newspaper. His tall, thin bride of nearly twenty years was flitting around the living room as if she was searching. Closets, drawers, and the oak chest were opened and closed more than once. From her antique rocker, Jake's grandmother Ginny watched curiously as well.

"Honey, have you seen our smaller photo album? I'm going to visit Lil Carter after lunch, and I wanted to show her some pictures of the kids." She stood above him where he was comfortably sprawled out on their forest green couch.

For fun, he briefly pretended he did not hear her, and then when he sensed her impatience with him he said, "My dear, it's right behind you. It's on the shelf." When she turned back around, he saw his wife's facial expression had shifted from exasperation to relief. She took the book down from the shelf and shared a moment with them.

"Here's a shot of Jake and Netty I want her to see." She pointed to the photo which captured them on their favorite rock. "They had no idea I was nearby that day. When they first began exploring, I was nervous, so I followed at a distance." She paused and smiled slightly as she adored the photo. "They're so good for each other. Don't you think?"

Dan McGee returned to his paper while uttering, "They're 13, Dear, not 31." He shook his head slightly in amusement.

"A mother can hope," a smiling Gramma McGee interjected. "Netty is perfect for Jake. I can just tell. Since your father's disappearance, Netty has become his new best friend." She watched her son peer over his newspaper again.

"It seems like yesterday. Doesn't it?" He began to think back to that part of his life, the many years before his dad's disappearance as well as those days during the search, but when he caught himself he tried to block the horrible memory out. His missing father and unanswered questions still hurt him too much. There were days when guilt riddled Jacob McGee's son, guilt about giving up. Dan was 43, and it still hurt to think about his father's disappearance.

Able to guess his thoughts, Jake's mom attempted to change the subject. "What are you reading about?"

"Local gossip and something else that might affect us."

"What's that?" Dan's wife asked curiously, relieved that she had so quickly eased his mind.

Her husband spun the paper around so she could read it with him. "Jake won't like it. I don't like it. My father would have hated it." He went on to explain how Crown Developers were the only bidders for a long-rumored branch or spur off of the Casey Highway. He explained how it might become a reality, and how it would most likely eliminate some of the state's game lands not too far from Honesdale's rural area near McGee property lines.

The article explained how the Pennsylvania Department of Highways had tossed about the Casey Spur Proposal for many years. If attempted and completed, it meant more jobs for an area that saw jobs hard to come by recently. That made it attractive to many folks despite the damage it would cause to the game lands. It meant more traffic on a highway designed to create a more direct route to the Catskills in New York. It meant dynamite and the destruction of forested lands. These were lands set aside for animals and folks like the McGees who loved nature.

Danielle gasped. "Oh no, Dan. Have you read the entire article?"

"Not yet. Why?"

She spun the Independent back in his direction and pointed to its second column. "Look who is promoting the construction."

His forehead wrinkled and then his eyes widened. "Codger Menke?" he asked himself in disbelief. "It's Codger Menke. Pop never trusted that lump of coal." Menke was famous county-wide for being the most controversial of the county's three commissioners, yet somehow he managed to achieve re-election. "I bet that deep down inside part of his reasoning is to spite my father. He'd dynamite everything. It's like the quarry thing all over again."

"That reminds me," Danielle told her husband. "The kids are exploring again today. Right now, in fact. They're to be home by dinner."

As she grabbed the keys and her photo album she added, "Please stick in the frozen pizza by five o'clock if I'm not back from Lil's house by then." She kissed Dan atop his head, teased him once again about his thinning hair, and she was gone before he could retaliate.

Getting lost in his paper once again he muttered to Jake's gramma, "Mom, what did she say about pizza?"

CHAPTER 9

"You never told me you were looking for him all this time!" Netty responded in a surprised tone as she sat upright upon their rock. "Where are you looking?"

Still feeling a little awkward about my confession, I stared off at some distant point. "Here in the woods." I turned to my newest confidante on this subject and added, "That has been my real reason for all of these explorations with you. I enjoy your company out here. We both like the same things, but most of all I have been looking for Gramps."

I was sure this was pretty heavy stuff for Netty, and she thought a while before resuming our conversation. Not too much time passed, and *she* was the one throwing stones. One of the perks to our friendship had always been the understanding that silence did not make either of us uncomfortable. After only a minute or two, she asked, "Do your parents know about this? Do they think or even hope he might still be alive?" Then she closed by asking, "What makes you think he's still alive, Jake? And why out here?"

I stopped looking for ticks by this point and stood up. Extending my hand to her I said, "Let's get going. We'll talk while we explore." Off we went, farther away from the stream than we ever ventured before. As we talked and explored, Netty occasionally marked a young maple tree with two squirts of fluorescent, lime-green spray paint. Each squirt resulted in a spot no larger than a quarter. She was careful and always left two marks first on what we thought was the *stream side* of the tree. Then she repeated a single mark on the opposite side, too. We both felt that marking trees was a good mapping technique that injured and defaced nothing.

When we finally reached the top of a ridge which we had casually hiked for a half an hour, I looked about. The view was not expansive, yet I was confident, and felt I knew our position in relationship to home. Looking back I retraced our steps and tried to get my bearings. Netty simply plopped on the ground and drank from her metal thermos. It was army style, complete with greenish camouflage fabric on the outside.

"Jake, let me see if I understand all of this." I leaned against a large maple tree and nodded for Netty to continue. "Six years ago your grandfather told your parents—"

"My grandmother. He told my grandmother."

"Whatever. He told her he was going for a hike. It was a normal day, not stormy or threatening. He just went for a walk out here in the woods."

I do not know why, but for a moment I became upset. "Yes! For the kajillionth time, Netty! Yes! My gramps loved being in these woods. To him they were *his* woods. After my 7th birthday, there were times when he'd bring me along.

We'd even bring Artie with us. In fact, he took Artie for hikes long before he started bringing me along." After I said it like I did, I felt terrible.

"That part I understand. So no one heard from him, and no one in any of the search parties ever found him or any traces of him out here. As much as it must have hurt, after a while your parents pretty much accepted the fact that he wasn't coming home."

Now I sat down with my back against one of the largest trees we had seen all day. I sighed. I snapped a twig and playfully tossed its remnants at Netty. "You can say the *d-word*, Netty. Yes, they have accepted his death." After a pause I added, "I haven't."

"Why not?"

I scratched my head. I felt bad about how I just snapped at her. "I told you this morning. I need proof. It's that simple. My grandfather wasn't feeble. He was 59, not 89. He wouldn't be careless. Something must have happened, and I want to know what that was." His voice had heightened.

Netty reached out and touched my arm. "Okay. Okay. Relax." She was calm. "I don't blame you, and I am flattered that you've finally told me about all of this." She began to get up from the ground when she indirectly issued a challenge. "But we're never gonna find him if all we do is sit here and talk about him."

I know my head snapped upwards as I understood what she was implying. Netty was willing to help! When the adults in my life might think I was coping poorly and other friends might say I was loony, Netty was willing to go the extra mile and help her friend find some answers if there were any answers to be found.

CHAPTER 10

Like two young explorers, we spent the afternoon checking out small rock formations that might have been cave entrances. We meandered in and out of various groves of trees that bordered fields or ponds which we were seeing for the first time in our lives. We seldom spoke; only when something of natural beauty caught our eyes. Even then we sometimes remained silent. Around midafternoon, Netty caught a glimpse of a doe and two fawns. They were not newborns, but they were small. Not wanting to startle them, she merely tapped my shoulder, put her finger to my lips, and pointed in the direction of the deer. Though the touch of her finger was odd, I nodded my appreciation without a flinch, and we moved on.

It is no wonder to me that people love the forest. The combination of the natural colors such as greens, yellows, and browns all accented by a beautiful blue sky on a clear day is magnificent. Sunlight accentuates everything it touches, painting a softer golden hue all around.

Not to go unnoticed are the sounds of the woods. I love hearing the raucous call of a crow, the rapid fire pop pop popping of woodpeckers, and the gentle trickling of water across century-old stones. Even the snapping of a branch upon which I stepped has its own distinct sound. Including the snorts of young deer like those we were fortunate to witness, the whole environment is full of the sounds of life in the wild. Blindfold me, and I can identify them all.

Finally Netty suggested we should head back for dinner. "Let's finish sketching the map, head home, and put on the final touches later." I nodded in agreement. While she watched me sketch, she made some suggestions, remembering details I had forgotten.

As she looked about, Netty spoke of the woods and its beauty. "Artie would love it here. Wouldn't he?"

I chuckled. "Oh I bet he would! He might be nonstop action. During those times when he'd accompany Gramps and me, we'd hear him more than see him out here."

Immediately Netty stopped what she was doing. She spun and looked down at me as I talked and mapped at the same time. I was smiling as I remembered the hikes with my grandfather. Her tone changed. "Jake, where was Artie the day your grandfather disappeared?"

"Huh?" I looked up at Netty wondering why she would ask.

"Where was Artie that day?"

I folded the map, stood, and zipped it into my backpack. The two of us always took turns wearing it. In the pack were first aid items, matches, a flashlight, a magnifying lens and a few other items we deemed prudent to have along. We even included a couple of flares. To light a fire, we even toted some steel wool and a small, nine-volt battery in the event the matches were wet and there was no sunlight for the magnifying glass. Such was the influence of Mrs. Keen's lessons. Netty suddenly looked mighty impatient. As I spoke, I handed her the backpack. It was her turn to carry it.

"Artie was with Gramps. At least I got Artie back."

Netty was suddenly so excited she could hardly contain her increased enthusiasm. I stepped back and watched her struggling with ideas and words. Finally she blurted, "Jake! Don't you get it?"

"Get what?" I had never seen her like this before. She was pacing back and forth across fallen logs and through some undergrowth. Her eyes were wide open, and she continued to speak.

"Artie might be able to lead us to your grandfather!"

CHAPTER 11

Netty's mother and Jake's mother had been friends since their elementary school days. Their friendship had been tried and tested several times over. "Danielle" and "Lil" were friends for life. Like schoolgirls and best friends, they dared to trust each other and share their dreams. They were confidantes, and some family members would suggest they could read each other's deepest thoughts. Their math teacher, Mrs. Crosby, used to teasingly warn the boys in her class. "Boys," she said, "the mind readers are the most dangerous kind of female! They don't even have to study for my tests!"

Back then during elementary school, they enjoyed the land of make believe. During recess they raced their classmates to their favorite cluster of trees where they let themselves pretend to be moms and daughters, doctors and patients, as well as singers and dancers. In those days, certain old trees outside the school were considered to be a better place to meet with friends, and it was there that Lil and Danielle liked to play. They would help each other learn the words to their favorite songs and together try to solve any boy problem that ever came up between them.

When time passed and they had us, more than once they looked back together and recalled being scolded by another teacher, Mr. Crum. Everyday Lil walked to school while Danielle had to ride a bus across town. Lil would faithfully await the arrival of Danielle's bus, so they could enter the school building together. One such day, Lil had forgotten some things she wanted to bring to school. After Danielle arrived, they innocently walked to Lil's house, returned to school a little bit late, and they encountered a stern Mr. Crum. He lectured them about *never* leaving the school property once they had arrived in the morning. Like Netty and I had become, as kids our own mothers were nearly inseparable. As adults that part of their friendship had not changed much at all.

On this day, while sipping decaf coffee and stealing one more cookie, Danielle mentioned to Lil what her husband had seen in the newspaper. "Dan thinks that a new branch off of the Casey Highway would destroy a lot of State Game Lands."

"How close to us might it be built? I would hate to see or even listen to a ton of traffic running through our area." They suspected such a project would affect both families equally.

"One thing Jack, Netty, and I like about our home is the quiet." As she expressed her concern, Lil smiled a devilish smile and pushed another cookie at Danielle.

"You're bad! Oh, all right. One more! I can't keep eating these!" She feigned a painful look as she picked up yet another chocolate chip delight.

Lil had heard of the Casey Spur plans before. As she got up from the kitchen table she said, "I wonder why it hasn't happened yet." She paused as she looked through her window at the land she loved. "I wonder if it ever will."

Working in the Wayne County Courthouse part time, Lil occasionally heard comments concerning highway work and other projects. She turned around and faced her friend. "To be honest, I haven't heard too awfully much about it lately."

Danielle sighed. "I hope it never happens." She joined her friend at the window as she took in the beauty of the outdoors that was northern Wayne County. The Carter's home offered a view that was rivaled by few properties in the area. The McGees had always admired it. In fact, Dan nicknamed the Carter residence *Sunset City*. Several gatherings which began as picnics on their back deck became opportunities to star gaze. All of them loved to watch the sun go down, enjoy the solitude, and wonder at the stars above.

Jack Carter pulled up the driveway in his old Dakota. Trucks were handy when people lived in the rural areas outside of Honesdale. Firewood was easier to collect, and large game was easier to transport, too. Lil's husband was an avid outdoorsman. He more than his wife was responsible for Netty's interest in what nature had to offer, although Lil Carter never gave anyone the impression that she was once a townie as a kid.

He walked in, gave his wife a kiss, and smiled. "Hi, Danielle! Eating all my cookies?" Jack sat with the ladies after he poured himself a tall, cold glass of milk. The chocolate chip cookies did not stand a chance. "Where's Netty?"

As if they were prompted, the two women simultaneously laughed and said, "With Jake!" More than once Dan McGee and Jack Carter suspected that their wives had dreams concerning their kids being together forever. Dan loved to tease Jack that paying for the wedding would be up to him. Jack always countered with a remark suggesting a "...jeans and tee shirt affair; not too much different than a barbecue!" That always caused a chuckle because Dan McGee was famous for his ability to cook over a barbecue pit.

"Jack, have you heard anything about the new highway project lately?"

He glanced at his wife with a surprised look on his face. "Here, Honey, have a look at today's Independent's front page." Right there, along with photos of Codger Menke, was a map of the proposed project. Under the map an article explained what the state of Pennsylvania's Department of Highways had decided to do. If the article could be believed, the new highway was soon to be underway, and it would eventually pass within ten miles of their homes.

CHAPTER 12

"How could I be so stupid?" I kept asking myself. Netty and I were nearly back to the stream. We chose to stop a minute at our original outpost, so we could catch our breath and collect our thoughts.

We both began tossing stones toward the stream and enjoying our creation of an occasional plop. "Jake, stop kicking yourself, and let's do some constructive thinking here. Soon we'll be home, and we might not have much private time to plan."

I knew she was right. Parents were parents. They always seemed to be asking annoying questions. I was excited at the thought that Artie might hold some of the answers to finding out just what had happened to my grandfather. As we returned from deep in the woods, we discussed the pros and cons of telling our parents our idea regarding Artie's role. Both of us finally agreed it was way too early to bring moms and dads in on this. In fact, we both feared that our parents might stop the search.

"Okay...okay. It shouldn't be too hard to pull off. We just start bringing Artie more often. That won't seem suspicious. Will it?" I looked up at Netty to see if she still agreed.

"I don't see that as a problem." She was out of stones to throw, so she turned toward me and continued. "However, there is one thing that does concern me."

"What?"

"If we turn Artie loose way out there," she said as she pointed in the direction from which we had just returned, "who knows where he'll lead us? We have to seriously consider it. I'm not knocking Artie, but he isn't the most obedient hound in the woods."

I began to stand up and checked myself for ticks. Some habits do not ever die. "I know, but thanks to a lesson my dad taught me, I've got that covered." I told her the story of my first solo adventure into the woods with Artie, and how I learned about dropping my shirt, jacket, or sweater as a marker. "We can bring a long rope leash, too."

"Well okay. We could try it. He's your hound. I guess we don't have much of a choice." She hopped up, and we started toward the stream. The afternoon sun in the forest was not quite as intense, and the stream's water was cool. Together the shade and stream were soothing after a day of hiking. We walked quite a while before we spoke once again.

"Think this will work?" I asked quietly as we neared the first open field on our property. "A lot of time has passed. How can I ever expect Artie to pick up a six year old trail?"

"Maybe he'll recognize something. Who knows?" Netty did not want to discourage me, her best friend, before I ever gave my dog a chance. "Yeah! That's it! We just take Artie in the general direction and follow his lead." Netty was trying to sound supportive. She climbed upon a stone wall and looked around as if she was an explorer overlooking a new territory. "Hey! Do you still have things that your grandfather gave you before he disappeared?"

"Sure! Lots of stuff. Why?"

Down off the wall she jumped and landed with a grunt. "Jake, Artie's a hound. Maybe, just maybe, he'll get a whiff of your grandfather and pick something up. It might not be a scent, but maybe it will trigger a memory."

We jogged off toward our pizza dinner that Mom had promised. Little did we know that dinner's success depended upon my father's memory.

CHAPTER 13

Commissioner Menke enjoyed the game of golf, and the threat of several days of rain by the end of the week had him headed to the course. It was not at all unusual to find him with family, friends, constituents, or businessmen playing in his foursome on a weekly basis. His home golf course was beautiful in its entirety. It was well-groomed, possessing slightly undulated fairways, while each was accented by stately sycamores and maples. Upon passing through the clubhouse gate, new arrivals were impressed by a brick, two-story, American Federal Style structure. The building was admired for its many arched windows accented by black shutters, as well as a clubhouse front entrance which was accented by a fanlight above its wooden double doors. The club was a nine-hole layout featuring scenic views, excellent playing conditions, and a top-of-the-line cocktail lounge where golfers enjoyed an excellent menu and drinks. The facility also boasted a banquet room that seated up to 150, a pro shop providing appropriate gear as well as state-of-the-art equipment, and conference rooms that were designated for more private matters. Codger Menke would wink at newcomers when he teased that *his* local course was a definite "home court advantage."

When David Crown joined Commissioner Menke for a round of golf one Tuesday afternoon in May, both men were meeting in person for the first time. Often Tuesdays were slow, so accommodating his request for a one o'clock tee-off time for a twosome was easy. Playing together out of the same electric cart offered both men a privacy they desired as well.

Golf was not their sole interest that day. Crown played the first card as they walked off the third green. "Well, Commissioner, what can you tell me about the highway project we discussed a while back?"

"What would you like to know, David?" The cart bounced as Codger's weighty frame landed roughly behind the steering wheel. They were off toward the 4th tee.

"It would help me to know whether or not there were other bids submitted," Crown openly admitted. He knew full well he was requesting some insight regarding privileged information, but he had heard from other businessmen that Codger liked it best when men shot straight from the hip.

Richard Menke smiled as he waved at a few folks on the fifth fairway to his left. And although his next comment to Crown was as accurate as Robin Hood's arrow, David Crown was more than a little uncomfortable hearing his golf partner ask, "Looking to save a bit of your money, Mr. Crown?" The President of Crown Developers was younger than Codger Menke by at least fifteen years and much less experienced when it came to private, unethical negotiations. Not wasting any time, the commissioner went for the jugular faster than

Crown ever expected. "What might you do with some of that cash you could possibly save by gaining such valuable information?" At that moment, in the middle of the fourth fairway, David Crown heard laughter he thought might be best described as evil drifting his way from the driver's side of the golf cart.

CHAPTER 14

Two days later there was no mistaking his anger. When Commissioner Kay opened Commissioner Menke's office door, Margaret saw it in his reddened face. In his hand was a rolled-up newspaper. If Menke's secretary had to guess, it was the Independent's most recent issue, and she knew why.

Before she could speak a polite "Good morning!", Kay briskly walked by her desk, opened Menke's door to his inner office, and just as quickly slammed it shut behind him. Margaret had no chance to alert her boss. Briefly she considered calling the office of the third and final commissioner, Elliot Chambers, but decided against it fearing that her boss might not want an audience to what she suspected was about to be discussed. No sooner had the wooden door slammed shut and its translucent glass rattled enough that thoughts of the thunder outside crossed her mind. Margaret heard Commissioner Kay begin his reproach of her boss.

"What in God's world were you thinking? Are you even thinking?" he screamed. "You can't make County decisions all on your own!" She heard no reply, but Margaret could easily imagine Menke's well-known, arrogant smirk and how it would only enflame Commissioner Kay's rage. "And this news release? This article? This time you have just gone too far!"

Finally Codger Menke's voice could be heard, and by his tone he sounded nearly apathetic while expressing his reply. "How dare you come in here like this? Who do you think you are?"

"How dare I?" Kay yelled in disbelief. "How? Are you crazy? We represent the people who put their faith in us to do things correctly! What you've done is ludicrous!" Margaret heard the newspaper slammed on a desktop. "You don't get to decide whether or not a highway gets built and where it gets built!" He finished his scathing rant with a stinging, final reprimand. "And you and your wallet *certainly* don't get to decide who builds a highway! I am so glad this is an election year!"

The younger commissioner did not wait for a rebuttal. As quickly as the event started it was over. Commissioner Kay opened Codger's inner door, exited, and slammed it one more time. Decent man that he was, he composed himself and looked at Margaret saying, "I'm very sorry you had to hear that."

Proof that perhaps she had been working for Codger Menke too long, she quickly shrugged and said, "It's okay. I didn't hear a thing," but to herself she silently wondered what ol' Codger had done this time to stir up trouble.

CHAPTER 15

For two, long, boring days thunder echoed and it rained enough to swell some nearby creeks. There was no way that my mom and dad would understand why I ever would want to go in the woods in such weather. No story I could conjure would sound feasible. I thought of several. My weakest was how I wanted to make sure the animals in the woods were safe! My dad really would have had a good laugh about that one. Netty showed up after lunch on the first day. She was equally frustrated, but she attempted to keep things going in a positive direction.

As she flipped through channels on my bedroom television, not really paying close attention, she began to ask questions. "Where are the things your grandfather left behind?"

"Here's one that's pretty cool." I pulled an old compass down off the shelf above my bed. "He tried to teach me how to use it, but I never quite go the hang of it." I tossed it to her.

"Cool!" Netty snapped open the lid atop the compass. She was surprised by its weight. "What else do you have?"

I explained how there were many things throughout the house. The fact that the house was once my grandfather's house meant that several items on display were actually Grandpa's or my dad's at one time. Most of the paintings downstairs, for instance, were collected by my grandfather. Most of them were pastorals.

"His favorite was that of a proud buck standing in the woods on a winter day. Another was that of a rabbit. He thought it was clever how the artist had blended the rabbit in with its environment. Grandpa always admired natural disguises.

"In our curio cabinet downstairs is a collection of old coins. He told me I could have them, but made me promise to never keep them hidden someplace or just put away in a dumb box in a closet or a drawer." Having witnessed it on another day, Netty knew that from the look on my face I was enjoying the memory, the telling of the tale.

"Gramps told me that each coin was worth very little, but that seeing them all together on display made them all the more impressive." I shared how Gramps McGee seemed to have a tale to go along with each of the coins. "I wish I could remember them." For a moment, I felt sad, realizing I had forgotten parts of what Grampa told me.

Netty sensed my sadness and quickly asked me to recall what I could.

"Well, one of the coins down there in the case came back with him from Africa."

"Really?" Netty responded quickly. She sensed my mood was on the upswing. "Your grandfather was in Africa?"

I began to sit up a bit. A sense of pride overtook me as I continued to talk about my grandfather's past.

"Yeah! Wait 'til you hear this! My grandfather was in the navy for a few years; four, I think. It was not long before my dad was born. He spent a few years on an aircraft carrier where he was assigned some sort of work upon the ship's deck. On the carrier he traveled quite a bit, but it wasn't until he flew with the navy that he got to Africa."

Now Netty's interest began to soar. "Your grandfather was a pilot?" She sounded shocked. "I never knew that –"

"Noooo!" I interrupted. "I said he flew *with* the navy. I didn't say he flew *for* the navy." Netty listened as I explained how my grandfather was a steward on board navy planes. "While in the navy he flew along with M.A.T.S. That meant *Military Air Transport Service*. My grandfather's job was to keep a record of cargo and know just exactly what was on board his plane."

I further explained that M.A.T.S. flew United Nations soldiers into dangerous missions in dangerous places. I included how they were peace-keeping missions, but they were still in danger nonetheless.

"Gramps once left the U.S. for Africa on one of seven transport planes. They were big, slow cargo planes." I was excited as I retold a story that my grandfather had shared with me years ago. "Only two planes returned safely."

"What happened?" Netty had stopped flipping channels and was now leaning forward eager to hear more.

"Five of the planes were sabotaged!" I stood up and looked out my bedroom window as I told the story. "The crews were exhausted by the long flight over the Atlantic Ocean. Once upon African soil, while the soldiers slept, an enemy slipped some bombs aboard five of the planes."

I told her more. "In the brief time Gramps was on the ground, he bought something, probably food. That's how he got the African coins that are displayed downstairs." Then I told Netty about my grandfather checking the cargo list or manifest only to find an unaccounted-for box. From the inside of the box my grandfather heard ticking.

"Gramps saw nothing on the list that should be ticking, so he tossed it out of the plane just after take off! Later that night, a co-pilot sheepishly admitted he had purchased a clock and forgot to report it to my grandfather."

I knew there were more stories, and gladly spent part of the afternoon telling them to her. As long as I was alive, stories regarding my Grandfather McGee would be passed along.

Netty finally decided it was time to go home for dinner. The annoying rain had let up enough for her to walk, but about the same time she was headed out of the door my dad came home from work. He offered to take her home, so I rode along with the two of them. When we arrived at the Carter's house, my dad climbed out of his truck to speak with Mr. Carter. It was a brief visit, but it was long enough for Netty to ask one more question.

"Can you think of any other stuff your grandfather left behind? We can't expect Artie to get many clues from what I saw today."

"Well, I'm sure there's plenty of stuff in the attic. We'll check it out tomorrow. Mom says it's supposed to rain anyway."

Netty smiled and told me that tomorrow she would be over to visit. We both knew we were going to be busy in the attic. "I'll bet there are plenty of stories up there!"

CHAPTER 16

Netty's mom dropped her off at our house the next day. The steady rain was a distraction as it pounded upon the roof above the attic. More than once we commented about how loudly the rain drops pelted the metal roof above our heads, but eventually the rainfall went unnoticed. Grampa used to say, "If you hang long enough, you'll get used to it."

We were surrounded by boxes. Some contained familiar items while others did not. Some of the dusty cardboard treasure chests were labeled. Others were not. When I told Mom we would be up in our attic, she asked me what we would be doing. "Just snooping around. We're bored. There's stuff up there that's just neat because it's old. That's all, Mom."

She smiled and requested that we do not leave the place a mess. "If you find anything valuable, don't tell your father. Tell me." We all laughed, and Netty took off up the steps. I was right behind her. The less we said, the better it went for us.

We were not there long when my partner had another good idea. "Let's bring Artie up here and see what happens."

I was all for the plan, but it turned out that Artie was not so keen on the idea. He had never been invited up there before. Eventually we cajoled him with a Milk Bone or two. Even then Artie seemed a bit uncomfortable being in the attic. However, in a few minutes he surprised the two of us.

As we opened a few boxes in search of memorabilia we could connect with my grandfather, Artie began nudging a box off in a corner we had not investigated. After a while, I noticed his behavior was repetitive. He seemed insistent upon nudging the box and pawing at it.

"Netty, look at Artie." I put down a box I was holding and watched my hound persistently nudge the old cardboard box. It had been tightly taped shut and was bigger than the tri-colored basset until he reared up and placed his front paws upon it. He actually began to whimper.

Netty was equally curious. "Do you think whatever's in that box belonged to your gramps?"

"Only one way to find out!" I whispered excitedly. I had brought along a penknife, and with that I carefully cut through the packaging tape that kept the large, khaki-colored box sealed. Then I noticed my grandfather's name upon the back side of the box.

"Good boy, Artie! You sure saved us a lot of time." We wouldn't have come across that part of the attic until later. "Good boy!" With his tail wagging back and forth, thwacking nearby cardboard containers, Artie seemed just as excited as we were.

Inside the dusty cardboard box were articles of clothing. At first, both of us wondered why the clothes were ever saved and not donated to some charity. They were not too worn or tattered, but they were not new either. Then we began to see a theme or a pattern to the items in the box. Each was some sort of clothing designed for hunting or fishing; items that Gramps had worn and, at the same time, items someone could wear again someday. I wondered if the articles of clothing had been saved for me. Perhaps Dad wore them at one time, and perhaps I would as well. I liked the idea.

"Look at this hat, Jake!" Netty thought it was odd looking and tried to stifle her giggle, for she did not want to offend me.

I just smiled at her. I was momentarily grateful that she was being considerate, then laughed aloud myself. The hat she held was leather on the outside, cottony inside, and had two ear flaps that tied at the top. She put it upon my head, and we both roared. Then the attic filled with quiet as I continued to look for more sentimental objects. I pulled out Grampa's red, plaid flannel shirt. With that and the fishing boots I found, I began to sense a connection...experience a flood of memories. Netty patted me on my back and asked if I was okay. I acknowledged that I was feeling weird, but I was indeed okay.

Artie barked! So intent were we in our search, we had forgotten all about him even being there among all the boxes and contents. When we looked at him we saw that he had one of Grampa's old mittens. He would not relinquish it when I reached for it. Artie backed away with a firm grip on his prize.

"I think he's made a connection," Netty whispered. She did not want to rile Artie, so she purposefully spoke in a soft voice. "It only makes sense. I bet your grandfather wore those while he was out walking with him."

"And I bet he would pet Artie from time to time while wearing those very same mittens." At that moment, I sensed that I was not the only one in the attic remembering my Grandfather McGee.

"I think our mission here is complete, Netty. Let's grab a few things." I pointed across some boxes. "Get that hat!"

We finished repacking the box and exited the attic. The stairwell was steep and narrow, so we had to be careful not to trip over the newest detective in the group. My mom had been making up beds when she heard the stairwell creaking as we descended to the second floor. Artie's pace was announced with traditional basset footsteps of *ker-thump, ker-thump, ker-thump* all the was down the attic stairs.

"Find anything? I thought you'd be up there longer."

"Just some of Grampa's old stuff. We repacked it." Then I added, "Don't worry, Mom. No treasures were discovered." But deep down inside we knew that what we discovered might have been pretty important stuff.

CHAPTER 17

Mom followed us down into the kitchen. Like normal kids, we were looking for something to eat. Meanwhile Mom leafed through the local paper and suggested we have a lunch. "We have to run to the mall one of these days for school shopping," she announced. "Sales are going on." With that she left the paper across the counter where we could see it.

I pretended to look at the sale ads to appease my mom. Netty scanned the front page. She stopped and stared intently.

"Jake, have you read this?"

"What?"

"This article says that a new branch of highway will likely be built soon, and it will run through some of the State Game Lands near us!" My mother heard her and turned around.

"Let me see that!" I read what Netty pointed out. I am sure that the look on my face indicated my enormous concern. "How can they do this? These lands weren't meant for highways." Then I read deeper. "Mom! Did you see this part? Codger Menke is partially responsible! Grampa never spoke a nice word about that man."

My mom looked first at me and then at Netty. "Netty, your mom, dad, and I were just discussing that recently. It's awful news."

As I stood I fidgeted. "This isn't right." The three-day rain was no longer our enemy. Crown Developers and my grandfather's nemesis had now moved from the back burner to the front. We felt more time, maybe a lot more time, would be required to discover answers about Grampa. It was time the Department of Transportation would not be willing to spare.

"Mom, can they do this? Do we have any way to stop them?" I paced around the kitchen, fists clenched and a worried look upon my face.

She took my shoulders in her hands. Gently she attempted to calm me. "Jake, the Carters, Dad and I plan on approaching the County Commissioners. There will be others with us. We hope to learn what can be done to prevent all of this."

"Mrs. McGee," Netty asked, "when can all of you meet with them? It sounds as if the project is almost a certainty."

"Your mother said she would check into it when she goes to work at the courthouse tomorrow. We might know very soon." Then my mother looked at me, and in a relaxed tone said, "Jake, let's not give up before we ever get started, and let's not borrow any worries." As she said it, the first sunlight we saw in days angled its way through the kitchen window, and I hoped it was a good sign.

CHAPTER 18

Netty and I met early the next morning, visibly excited thanks to more bright sunshine. Too, we were motivated by the local news.

"What has the two of you so bubbly today?" my mother inquired playfully as we hustled about her kitchen, grabbing fresh-baked cookies, making peanut butter and jelly sandwiches, and stocking up on water bottles from the refrigerator. I dropped the first bottle to the floor as I attempted to fill Netty's canteen for her.

"Whoa, Mister McGee!" my mom teased.

"Sorry, Mom," I said as I began nervously mopping the tile floor with a handful of paper towels. "After all the rain, we just have big plans, and we're anxious to get started." I looked at Netty for support. Netty could sell my mother anything. She could probably sell a lawn mower to a boathouse resident.

"We're exploring new places today out passed the big rock. By the way, my mother showed me the great photo you took of us. It's cool!" Having increased the smile on my mom's face, Netty tugged my arm and led me outdoors. Mom thought Netty was cute when she took me in tow, and was even more happy when she noted that Artie was being taken along with us.

Once we were at the edge of McGee land, it was not long before we three adventurers felt the coolness of the woods. The trees somehow seemed more quiet and relaxing. At the same time, on this new day, the forest offered exciting possibilities. With Artie still on his leash, Netty and I quickly hiked to our most remote outpost, finally stopping to rest.

"Okay. This is it." Here I was, the grandson who would not give up. I scanned the immediate area. I loved the scent of the forest and the hints of yellow morning sunlight that painted the thick tree trunks of the forest as well as their branches laden with needles or leaves. With a bit of trepidation I asked my partner, "Are we sure we should do it this way?"

My doubts seemed to cling to the sunbeams cascading through the gaps between the trees all around us. These doubts regarding our agreed-upon plan had developed during the past two rainy days and were eating at me. I wondered if Netty felt the same.

She was patient. She spoke softly when she replied, "Jake, he's *your* hound now. Your grandfather trained him, but if you suspect Artie will not come home–"

"No. He *will* come back. I just know it." Whatever doubts I experienced had evaporated. With that being said, I knelt to Artie's side. As per our plan, I presented my basset hound who was once my grandfather's basset hound, with some of

Grampa's old clothing articles he had not sniffed since his master's disappearance.

For a moment, I thought to myself how much time I spent searching the woods and never once thought that Artie could have been out here with me. Briefly I thought to myself that I had wasted all that time. Then I passed it off as nonsense, knowing I'd done what I could. I looked at my hound, took a deep breath, and wondered what was about to happen.

We had no way of knowing whether or not Artie would recognize his masters's scent, or even if there was a scent to be recalled. It was a long shot. Nor did we know what would take place once I unclipped Artie's leash from his collar. Would he move away slowly and methodically, or would the powerful, low-to-the-ground hunter bolt, employing his howl to call out to us, "Follow me!"

CHAPTER 19

I released the clasp at the end of Artie's leash, and my hound was free. Nothing happened. A minute passed and then another. So quiet and still were the first few minutes that the flutter of birds all around us was a distraction.

What we witnessed at first was not at all what we expected or had hoped. Our basset partner continued to stand unaffected by his freedom, seeming to have not a care in the world. Was this how Grampa had trained him? I wondered how to set him in motion.

Casually Artie continued to gaze left and right. Occasionally he followed the movement of the tiny, brownish-streaked sparrows above us that were hopping from branch to branch.

I was unsure as to what I was expecting, but what looked like apathy was not it. Artie's failure to begin the hunt was a disappointment of a far greater magnitude than the time I learned I had lost a class election, learned my frog had died, and even greater than when I learned my favorite baseball player was out of baseball. That one really hurt, and at that moment, Artie was surpassing even that. Let me pause here to take you down a rabbit trail.

Along with my cousin Alex and his parents, I once traveled from their home in D.C. to Pittsburgh on a train called the *Capitol Limited*. We opted not to ride the entire 790 miles to Chicago, for it was the city of Pittsburgh we wanted to visit and take in a Pirates game. The *Capitol Limited,* with its stainless steel exterior, consisted of a baggage car, transition dormitory, two sleeping cars, a dining car, a Sightseer Lounge, and two coaches. Each passenger upon the train enjoyed his or her own recliner along side a huge, plate-glass window. Such a trip!

Upon check in, we were thrilled to learn that the New York Mets were lodging in our hotel as well! Being an avid fan, I recognized several players as they walked through the hotel lobby from time to time. However, Sebastian Cort, a rookie player who had just been summoned from the minor leagues, was alone as he walked through. On a whim, I spoke to him as he passed.

"Hi, Mr. Cort," I said in a shy voice. "Good luck with the Mets." He smiled and proved to be quite pleasant.

"Hi," he returned in a gentlemanly manner. "I'm surprised you know who I am. Only with the Mets since last week, you know."

"I know." I pointed at my cousin who had been sitting beside me awestruck. "We're not from Pittsburgh. Alex lives in D.C., and I actually live in Eastern Pennsylvania about two hours from Citi Field. I see your games on television regularly."

"Mets fan? In Pittsburgh? That's so cool!" His smile was infectious.

I told him about our trip on the train and how the next day we were headed on to Chicago.

"Where are your folks?" he asked. "Your mom and dad?"

I explained I was with my cousin Alex, who by now had started breathing again. I introduced him to Sebastian. Then I introduced myself.

"His parents are up in the room for a minute. We are getting ready to visit the Carnegie Museums."

Then he shocked us! "Listen, I have to get going to the park, but how would the four of you like to see the game tonight? I'll leave my tickets for all of you at the Will Call Window."

At that moment, Alex's parents came out of the elevator. It's a good thing they did, for I had no idea what a Will Call Window was.

I excitedly introduced them to Sebastian who explained about the tickets if they were interested. They told him they would love to see the game that night, and shook my *new* favorite player's hand. Later that night we met him behind the Mets dugout and posed for several pictures of him standing with us.

Unfortunately just as that emotional roller coaster went up, it went down even more quickly. After a successful two-week stint with the club, he suddenly was injured crashing into an outfield wall. That was a huge disappointment, for we never saw him play in the majors again. His injury was career-ending. To me, that was a tremendous disappointment, and now we are back to my dog.

My disappointment in Artie's inability to understand what I wanted him to do was even greater than previous disappointments, for he seemed to have no intention to help find Gramps. For six years I hoped to find out *something*, get some answers as to what happened that summer afternoon, and my hopes sky rocketed at Netty's suggestion. Now my hound was seemingly useless.

Lucky for us, grandfather had a lot of riddles and sayings for various situations. One of them was, "K.I.S.S." or "Keep It Simple, Son." With that, I had an idea.

"Artie, find Grampa. Go find Grampa!"

Unbelievable! The roller coaster was back on track. As if he understood and was eager to please, my dog started off at a leisurely trot. Head down, moving side to side as he sniffed the forest carpet, it was evident to Netty and I that Artie was going to be thorough in his investigation, but it was equally evident that the investigation or hunt might be slow-going.

Our primary fear was that Artie would never find Grampa McGee's scent at all. Not anyplace. It would make for a long day in the woods. Our other fear was that he would find it, and suddenly he would take off, leaving us unable to maintain his pace. If we had to choose, we wanted to deal with the latter.

Artie moved on at a leisurely trot. The game lands were serene. Sunlight splashed through the branches and onto the mountain laurel below. Their waxy, dark green leaves shined and proved to be no obstacle for the hunter, but they were a challenge for Netty and me. Mountain laurel branches grow thick and are made of sturdy stuff, so following my hound was not always easy. At one point, Netty looked back and said to me, "I'm glad we didn't wear shorts!"

Shadows danced upon the ground to the tune of a gentle breeze. By noon the air was still, and the dance had come to an end. The forest was warm. And the quiet? Far from being a silent place, the trees were full of life from top to bottom. All of what was the forest environ composed a natural song; solitude the result. This atmosphere helped us be at ease, for the forest was everything Grampa Jacob said it was, and it was why he cherished each visit. He passed his love for the land on to me, and now Netty was loving it more, too.

Artie began leading us down what was once a logging trail, another nearly-forgotten piece of Wayne County history. One hundred and fifty years ago or more the path we followed was an entrance and exit for teams of horses pulling skids; empty going into the woods and loaded with logs on the return trip. Logging was of vast importance to many during the 19th century. First came the mills, and then came the stores and then more homes. Wood was in demand.

Roughly fifteen feet across, the old trail had become partially camouflaged by more-recent vegetation, rotted branches, and years of decayed leaves. Despite the decades that passed after logging had been abandoned, the trail Artie was inspecting was still recognizable. Moving along behind him was a challenge, but we hoped not an impossible one. As he waddled along, I imagined my grandfather walking this very path, and it made me smile.

Netty broke the silence between us. "Do you think he's on to Grampa's scent?"

I liked how my best friend called *my* grandfather "Grampa", as if he were her own. "He's certainly on to something," I replied matter-of-factly. "I just hope we're not following rabbit trails or creating the equivalent to one."

She looked at him quizzically. "What do you mean?"

We kept following Artie as I attempted to explain. "Well, he is a hound. They do chase rabbits." I paused to think and then said, "My dad had a friend from Georgia, and his friend used to label lengthy stories *rabbit trails* because they seemed to go all over the place before coming to the end. And the end of the trail? It might well turn out to be right where a person began, because that's what rabbits do. They circle back."

"So you think Artie might discover and follow other scents, we might be led all over, and he could lead us along unnecessary paths." Then she added, "Hopefully our exploration will come to an acceptable end."

I stopped my walking. I looked at Netty and said, "Yup. It's a possibility. We might be part of an adventure with lots of twists and turns." Then I asked an important question. "You still on board with this?"

CHAPTER 20

As the kids secretly explored and placed their hopes on Artie's memory and sense of smell, Lil Carter was at work in the courthouse trying to learn what she could about the proposed highway project which threatened the sanctity of State Game Lands not far from her home. Lil was a part-time secretary in the office of the Magistrate, located on the first floor not far from the well-guarded main entrance of the grand, old, red-brick building.

Prior to the 70's, the entrance of the courthouse was never guarded at all until an episode involving a divorce hearing and a deranged ex-husband changed all of that. Margaret Card McCovey decided she had suffered enough of her husband's abuse. After filing for a divorce and finally getting her day in court, her emotional presentation to the judge graphically recalled all she had been through. Her sobbing accentuated her tale as it echoed through the cavernous, high-ceilinged arena located upstairs above the lobby.

Of course, her soon-to-be ex-husband Tom was present, and he remained silent throughout most of the proceedings.

He spoke only when required, probably thinking the writing was on the wall. When he did speak, he was sullen, bordering on disrespectful. He gained no favor with the judge.

Upon hearing the Court's decision regarding the divorce, Mr. McCovey finally spoke up loudly saying, "You have not heard the last from me!"

Moments later as everyone in attendance walked down the courtroom's rear entrance stairwell toward the lobby and main entrance's arched doors, a fresh start awaited them. That all changed in an instant when Tom McCovey screamed at Margaret. Unfortunately rather than ignoring him, she reacted by turning around, only to find him pointing his pistol at her just before he fired.

She screamed pitifully, fell to the floor, and onlookers scattered. Only a few county employees ran toward McCovey in a brave attempt to subdue him. A collective gasp immediately filled the hall as he turned his gun on himself and took his own life. Margaret survived her stomach wound, but her life was never the same.

Since then, a metal detector was installed and armed officers were assigned. After passing through the device just inside the entrance, many of Lil Carter's county coworkers stopped by daily to chat since her office door was nearly always open. On days when she ate her lunch in the courthouse cafeteria, she would visit the folks she had not seen walking up and down the corridor. On sunny days when Lil shopped in stores along Main Street or went for a walk through the town square located along Court Street across from the County Courthouse, she chatted with more people she knew. Friendly by nature, Lil had a lot of folks in her corner.

One long-time courthouse friend was Jane D'Amore, the Clerk in the office of the Tax Claim Bureau, a friendly, pretty woman with vast responsibilities. Lil heard Jane's voice as she finished a phone call.

"How are you, Lil?"

"Hi, Jane! I'm good today. And you?" Her big smile was infectious.

Jane smiled in return and took a deep breath as she leaned against the tall door to Lil's office. "I'm pretty good, but things are busy upstairs," she said as she tilted her head upward in the direction of the Commissioners' offices.

Without knowing it, Jane had piqued her friend's interest. As promised, Netty's mom had her radar up, and although Jane was an unexpected reporter, Lil had always felt Jane was a responsible and reliable news source around their workplace.

"Oh it's this new highway thing," Jane replied. "From what I hear, not all the commissioners are on board with it. I think Commissioner Menke is pushing for it, but Commissioner Kay sits at the other end of the rainbow."

"What do you mean?"

"You know Cindy in Bureau of Elections. She told me she recently overheard yelling about the project." Again Jane sighed. "Mr. Kay is such a good guy. He has proven over the years that at least *he* has a code of ethics we can all admire. Have you ever met him?"

"I know who he is. We've exchanged greetings when he walks by here from time to time. Seems nice." Secretly Lil was happy to hear that just maybe there was hope. Maybe Commissioner Kay was someone the Carters, the McGees, and others would find approachable; a commissioner who might take up their cause.

CHAPTER 21

After we had negotiated a gradual, lengthy rise on the old logging trail, everything we saw that morning was new to us. In every direction, Mother Nature provided pristine, new scenes. As we walked, we pointed things out to each other so nothing was overlooked. Both of us wanted to share in the beauty of the game lands equally.

I have given more thought to the cycles of nature than most people, I guess. They are one of my favorite things about life. I always feel I miss something special when I don't see geese migrating in the spring or the fall. I love how some creatures, big and small, hibernate while others do not. Think about it. A 600 pound bear curls up and rests in a cave through every winter, returning in the spring, a sole example of one natural cycle. Yet a five ounce snowbird or "junco" lives outdoors year around, completing a cycle all its own.

Each year wildflowers come and wildflowers go, making room for next year's crop. The sun comes up, and the sun goes down daily, but every day the amount of sunlight we enjoy abates or increases for six full months. That's a cycle within a natural cycle. Too, I watch the Big Dipper as it seemingly rotates around Polaris each night against the beauty of an indigo sky spangled with sparkling white stars.

Then there are the leaves in the forest. Largely absent all winter, they open up to us each spring, blossom as summer's green arrives, and then they treat us to a spectacular show when, as the cycle continues, they splash the forest and countryside with their brilliant fall colors. I spoke of all this as we continued our hike, sharing my passion for nature with Netty. She agreed completely.

"It's no wonder Grampa enjoyed his hikes back here," Netty whispered. "He really knew what he was talking about."

"Yeah, he did." I stopped a moment. I could still see Artie in a clearing a bit off to our left, just meandering along a crumbling stone wall, hopefully having some success at finding a lead in Grampa's direction. "I wish you met him."

"Me, too," she sighed. "Hey...let's grab a bite."

We shared our P B & J's and some water, all the while watching Artie and looking about the woods.

"You never met him, but you would have liked my grandfather," I said after we had resumed hiking. I pushed some low-hanging branches out of the way as Netty passed. "He was full of fun, and not everything was about the woods."

"Tell me more," she politely insisted. I guess she sensed that I needed to share my memories, and she was more than a little interested.

I felt a smile cross my lips as I recalled one of my favorite memories about the man. A rabbit trail was in the making.

I spoke softly as we followed shoulder-to-shoulder behind Artie down another gentle slope. Occasionally our shoulders would touch, and I thought that was nice. In the distance, the stream could be heard cascading over some rocks. After two days of rain, streams were swollen.

"During the summer before second grade, my grandparents spent a few days with us in town. It was just before we moved here. That's how I can remember it." I leaned against a maple, the sun warming my face. Netty stopped a few feet ahead, still watching Artie off in the distance.

"Gramma and Grampa headed back here late the last evening."

"You mean back to their house."

"Yes, back to their house. My parents and I turned in for the night." I paused because I was savoring what I was about to share. I even chuckled.

"Things started happening at midnight, because that is when the first alarm clock sounded. Gramps had hidden it in the bathroom! Then fifteen minutes later we heard a second alarm all the way from the top of the hutch in the dining room!"

Netty's face was in full-smile mode by now. "Were there more?"

"We were sure there would be, so Dad and I looked and looked. No luck. Nothing." I went on to tell how all three of us laughed, of course, but also how we really could not sleep well since we were waiting for a third.

"So he set off two alarm clocks just to tease you?" She giggled at the idea.

"Oh trust me! There was another! He hid the third one in our linen closet along the hallway. It was an old-fashioned wind-up clock that required no cord. It clanged and clattered at six in the morning. Ever hear an old-fashioned wind-up clock? It is *really* loud!"

"No wonder you would like to find out what has happened to him. Sounds as if he was a character." Netty paused and said something that pleased me very much. "Sounds like he was kind of like you."

CHAPTER 22

Shortly after the sun had reached its noonday position, when the creatures of the forest seemed to settle and even disappear as if taking part in their own midday siesta, Artie began zigzagging much more quickly. Suddenly he bolted, and the chase was on!

I did not have time to look back. I could only hope Netty would be sure-footed enough to keep up. I should have known better. She blew by me like an arrow in flight. By now, she had grown to be more athletically built with longer arms and legs. No longer was she short in stature, but she did still have that long hair of hers flying behind her as she ran. There was no talking or yelling, only short, quick gasps and powerful footfalls. She ducked under branches. I ducked under the same, not missing a beat. Netty set a good pace, and I became her shadow.

Artie began his baying at a volume that woke up the woods. Birds scattered everywhere, twittering nervously enough for me to actually notice their increased level of excitement, equal to that of our tri-colored wonder we were attempting to

follow. Were they cheering for him in some sort of animal/
bird language? As we ran, I watched him ignore three deer
he had spooked, sending them hopping and dashing down a
tree-lined embankment.

We saw him. We lost sight of him. Into the sunlight,
out of the sunlight and right back in it again. The moment
came when we only heard him, followed by a flash of his white
hindquarters as he penetrated low, dark-green ground cover
that grew upon the bank above us. Against a backdrop of
chocolate-brown earth and decayed leaves, we glimpsed him
racing out on the other side like a torpedo. Howling all the
while, we relied more on his call to direct us than we did
watching his movements. Completely spent, I had to stop
and catch my breath. I was sweating crazily, my shirt clung to
my skin, perspiration dripped from my chin, and I sucked in
deep gulps of air as I bent over with my hands on my knees.
Now nearly six feet tall, my thick legs felt like old, cement
anchors that held me back, not the youthful tools of propul-
sion they were meant to be. I had chased Artie before, but
never like this. I was glad my hair was short so I was not
unbearably hot.

Netty? Netty kept going! She was amazing. She must
have sensed my lagging behind, for she began calling to me
as she described where she was headed in her pursuit of our
hunting machine. Attempting to leave a verbal trail was the
first that either of us had spoken since the event had begun. I
knew I had to catch up to her or risk losing contact with both
of them, and somehow I found the will to set out again, heart
pumping while ignoring any rocks and fallen trees in my path.

Just over the top of a ridge, a deep, open hollow appeared below me, and for an instant I saw my basset. He stopped and stood still becoming a statue, perhaps making a decision. Turning his head, he gazed down the hollow to the right and then quickly in the reverse direction. He did this twice and then took off again to the left, seeming to call to us both, "This way!"

As I chugged down to the bottom of the clearing, I discovered my partner positioned for rest as I was earlier, sweating like I had been doing, hands on her knees and sucking the same much-needed breaths of air.

"Don't stop!" she panted and waved me on. "I'll take your place when you tire out!"

Somehow I immediately understood her intentions. I began calling out to her what I was witnessing before me as well as where I was headed. We had become a team performing a necessary, high-speed kind of leap frog or relay race through the woods on a nature course we had never explored before. Just how long we could keep this up was anybody's guess. All I could think of was, "This is actually working! We're going to find my grandfather!"

CHAPTER 23

Equal to the haste with which the chase had begun, it came to an abrupt end. After taking several turns to catch my breath and start anew, with Netty not too far behind, I came upon Artie almost by accident. He had simply stopped and rolled to his side in some shade. He was panting, but otherwise he seemed to be relaxed and carefree regarding his surroundings. I poured some water from my canteen in the hopes that he would drink. He did. Not that he seemed to require any unusual attention, I stroked his side thinking it might help him to relax, and it seemed to work.

I could hear Netty getting closer, and when she arrived she asked the obvious. "What happened? I didn't hear either of you anymore and only guessed that this is where you'd be."

"I came around those pines back there," I said pointing behind her, "and this is where I found him. I don't think he's hurt. I think he just suddenly stopped."

We looked in every direction, and our eyes were telling our brains that we were witnessing something new. We had covered a lot of ground over the past hour, but neither of us felt as if we had become lost. There was just a feeling of newness to the area. For the most part, it was beautiful in an ordinary way, meaning the shaded ground ahead of us was relatively flat, easy to observe since the trees where not quite as thick as the stand of pines to our rear.

"Ever been here before," she inquired, "with your grandfather?"

As I poured more water for Artie I shook my head. "I don't think so. Are you ok?" I offered her a drink, too.

Netty was as red-faced as I, but otherwise she was no worse for the wear. "I'm okay, but that was really some chase." Nodding at Artie she said, "I wonder why he stopped right here."

"Let's look around, but first let me tie Artie to that sapling." From my pack, I pulled out a fifty-foot piece of clothesline I had coiled for easy transport and secured my hound to a nearby maple about three inches thick. "He's not going anyplace now."

It was as pretty as a wooded scene could get. Though not as abundant, there were trees of various heights and stages of growth. Only maples were plentiful as were the pines we passed moments ago. Hemlock trees and mountain laurel shrubs in full bloom were present, but not so thick to cut off our view of the surrounding area. Behind us boulders partially covered in deep, green moss cropped out from the banks of the hillside we had just descended. All the rocks were spackled with white and gray lichen.

"There has to be a reason he led us here," I hoped out loud. "Don't you think?"

"Yes, there must be. Keep your eyes open wide. Pay attention to details," she advised as we began exploring in a back-and-forth pattern. All the while Artie just relaxed.

"Believe it or not," I admitted, "after all that running I am almost afraid to go too much further."

Netty nodded in agreement. "I hope we haven't bitten off more than we can chew, Jake." The tone in her voice sounded uneasy.

Wanting to reassure her, I tried to sound confident. "Don't worry. I can get us back. We have lots of daylight."

"Yeah, I know," she said looking at her watch. It's only a little after two.

"Two?" I asked.

"Yeah, why?"

"That means we were on the run for nearly *two* hours." I chuckled a nervous chuckle, but I was beginning to doubt if we could return back home by carefully retracing our steps in less than two or three hours. I did not want Netty to know my worrisome thoughts at that exact moment, but I *was* concerned. Her voice brought me out of my reverie.

"Jake, look over there!" She pointed down a uneven bank. "Is that a bridge? A small stone bridge?"

I saw it. Right in the middle of all the forest, in the middle of the most unlikely of places, she had discovered a bridge. It had the look of field and river stone combined, arching to a maximum of about ten feet in the middle.

"Why in the world would a bridge be there?"

Which is what *I* was wondering. We moved in its direction gingerly. I do not know why, but I sensed we were both a bit leery. I guess it was the element of mystery associated with finding a bridge in a *very* unexpected location. We stepped carefully in its direction.

Then as if it had appeared out of nowhere, we were astonished at the sight of the largest rabbit either of us had ever seen! It was nearly two feet tall and looked like it weighed nearly fifty pounds. Artie saw it as well, yet for no explainable reason, no howling began anew. I wondered how that could be. Was my hound intimidated? In awe, we watched it wander about briefly and then vanish!

In microseconds, a lot went through my mind. Had we just spent the better part of two hours chasing a monster rabbit? Did we both witness such a creature? Of course, we did! Did all of this excitement have nothing to do with finding Gramps, but instead was it all about a gigantic rabbit? I experienced frustration, but I could not be angry. Artie had done what any hound would do.

"What was I thinking?" I dejectedly whispered to myself. I took a deep breath, let it escape, and to Netty I said, "Let's head back home."

CHAPTER 24

The journey home went more smoothly than anticipated. Hiking back through the woods, we began to realize that Artie had led us not in a straight line, but in a crisscross pattern, so we were not as deep into the State Game Lands as we had imagined. We decided it would be best if we kept Artie on the rope leash, and he did not seem to mind as he easily kept pace with the two of us, never trying to lead us in any other direction.

We ambled across the back of our property, and Dad saw the three of us first. He signaled with a friendly wave, and that was a relief because we had been gone about an hour longer than we had originally planned. Gramma saw us next as she came out the back door onto our veranda.

"Well look who decided to come home!" she called jokingly. "They must be hungry at last." She gave us both a hug as we climbed wearily up the steps and headed into the kitchen.

Over some of my grandmother's famous pot pies, all five of us chattered about our day. Artie was out like a light atop his bed in the kitchen corner. He certainly deserved some down time.

Mom spoke of how such days of summer reminded her of when she was a girl swimming with friends in a pond. "We did the whole tire-on-a-rope thing, until I broke the rope!" Then she added, "I was reminded about *that* many times by my friends. I was the featherweight in the group, and I was teased about breaking it."

Dad looked at Gramma and said, "Mom, remember how we'd hop in Dad's truck and go tubing in the Delaware?"

I was truly astounded and burst out, "What? Gramma and Grampa rode tubes down the river?"

"Jake McGee," she laughed, "I was young once, too!" My grandmother looked at Netty and smiled. "Miss Carter, don't you let Jake grow up thinking all that girls do is cook and clean."

"Oh don't you worry about that, Mrs. McGee. I think I crushed that idea a long time ago." Netty turned and looked at me. "Go ahead, Jake. Tell her about the bugs we caught for Mr. Mac. Who *really* caught the most?" We all laughed, because we all knew the answer.

Later that evening I had been recording on our map what I could from memory. It was no easy task, and I knew I needed Netty to check my notes at some point, and the sooner she did it the better the map would be. An unusual thought popped into my head, so I called her.

"Hello?" I heard her say into the phone. I pictured her in her bedroom, almost certain the day's events were still near the front of her mind.

"Hi," I said. "It's me." For a little more privacy, I closed the door to my room softly.

"Hi. What's up, Jake?"

I went into a short explanation describing what I had been doing minutes ago, and told her I wanted to ask her a question.

"Okay go ahead," she replied.

"I'm not quite sure how to phrase this." I paused. "Of all the people you and I know, who would you expect to worry most about the hours we spend in the woods?"

"What?" As I expected, she was taken by surprise by my question.

By now I was in my bean bag chair. "Think about it. Who do *we* know who was most affected by Gramp's disappearance?"

"Well that's easy. Your family."

I asked her to narrow it down.

She thought a moment and replied, "Your grandmother, I guess. She lost her husband, but your dad lost his father, too." I let her think on it. "Okay. I guess I'd say your grandmother has—"

"Bingo! That's what I thought." And then I went to explain why this was on my mind. "Netty, think about this afternoon when we returned from our adventure with Artie. We were late. We weren't late by a lot, but we were late."

"So what are you saying? What's your point?"

"Netty, Grampa disappeared while he was in the very same woods. Don't you think it would be natural for her to be a little bit worried about that same thing happening to us?"

Dead silence. Then, "I think I understand where you're going with this." More silence at her end. "This afternoon she showed no signs that she was at all concerned. You think that's odd. Am I right?"

"Exactly. I never thought about it before." By now I was standing again and looking out my window over our yard partially hidden in twilight. "And to be fair, six years have passed."

"Yeah, that's true. But when you think about it, if one of us fell off a ladder and broke a leg, wouldn't we always be leery of climbing a ladder again?"

The seriousness of the two events hardly compared, but I understood what she was saying which meant to me that she was in agreement with me. "I don't know. I just find it strange."

We agreed my grandmother was a wonderful and strong-willed individual. Many others in her position might have fallen apart, given up on life. She did not. She still worked around the house doing things that helped all of us. Perhaps she found comfort in us and purpose while keeping herself busy.

"Jake, have you ever talked to her about Grampa's disappearance?"

"No. I've wanted to talk. I even thought it might comfort her, but it's been so long now that I fear bringing it up again." By this time I was sitting at my desk.

"It might help you, too, Jake." Silence. Now the conversational ball was in my court.

"I guess you're right. We'll see." We talked about a few other things after that, and agreed that both of our schedules were filled for the next few days. I did remember to suggest she jot down things she wanted to add to our map. "We don't want to forget what happened today."

"Jake," she said in a half-chuckle, "I don't think that's possible."

CHAPTER 25

For a handful of days, various commitments kept us apart, so Netty decided to stop by our house. Mom and Dad were shopping, and Gramma was inside watching the local news. That evening while sitting on the porch where unsuccessful, tired volunteers had checked in years ago, I felt the urge to share with Netty more of what I had never shared with anyone before.

"Netty, believe it or not, I have more I want to tell you."

"What?" She looked startled. Perhaps she thought I'd used up all my surprises.

"Something has been happening in my head, and it takes place at the strangest times. It's not a voice, nor do I hear anyone calling. It's more like a silent signal that interrupts my thoughts." Netty could tell I was frustrated trying to explain to her something that I had long kept inside.

"Tell me about when it happens," she prodded. "Go into more detail."

I looked around as I struggled to describe my most private of all experiences. I chose Netty to be the first to learn about this part of my life, because she had never once been judgmental.

"It has happened in school, when I've been biking, and even when I was giving Artie a bath." I shrugged my shoulders. "There's no set time. It's just weird."

"Tell me what it feels like." She was looking right into my eyes, and as always it was clear that she was sincerely interested. As I looked back at her, it was not at all awkward or uncomfortable. For a second, I thought she was pretty. "Jake!"

"What?" I shook my head as if clearing it.

"I said, 'Tell me what it feels like.' "

Maybe I blushed a little. I don't know. I regrouped. "Sorry. I zoned out for a minute."

Again I hesitated. For all the times I think I had been telepathically prodded or interrupted by what I hoped might be my grandfather's silent signals, never before had I focused on it at length, and I *never* talked about it with anyone. I did not want to be labeled "crazy".

"Okay. I'm just going to say it. I sense that Gramps is trying to contact me." I stood up, perhaps because I was nervous telling my best friend such a thing. "There's nothing scary about what I experience. I don't feel guilt or fear, but I feel as if I am being reminded that there is more to be learned about my grandfather's experience, and he's the one telling me."

"Are you being told not to give up?"

"Yes. Actually it is *like* that, but words aren't being spoken."

Off in the distance a few cars passed by. A horn honked recognition, and we casually waved.

Softly Netty said, "It sounds kind of like waving a flag. Flags don't speak, but they surely give off a message."

"Exactly!" I replied. "It's like he's waving a flag, and he wants to be noticed."

The TV was playing. Its words drifted over the air in our direction. I shared with Netty that from time to time I felt guilty when I was not actively seeking my grandfather or his signals.

"It feels good to tell someone this," I said to her softly.

"I'm honored that you chose me," was her reply. "May I say something about this?"

"Sure." I was hoping she would have some insight.

"I wouldn't let it bother you too much," she said. As she said it she put her hand in mine. She *never* did that before.

"Let what bother me?" I must have sounded really stupid, for her eyes widened a bit when I asked.

"The whole guilt thing," Netty explained while she continued to hold my hand. "Let's pretend for the sake of discussion that Gramps is trying to signal to you."

"Okay."

"Jake, if he's actually sending signals, then that means he is aware that you are still looking." She gave her words time to penetrate my thick scull. "He knows you haven't given up hope."

I have to admit that her words made me feel a bit better. But the hand-holding thing? I *really* liked that! Suddenly it was quiet.

That is when we heard a *third* voice! It freaked us out until we realized it was Gramma.

"You two have room for me out there with you?"

Immediately Netty let go of my hand. I think she was embarrassed.

"Whoa! You startled us, Mrs. McGee!" Now we were both standing and opening the door for her.

"Gramma, how long were you standing there?" I asked sheepishly.

"Long enough," she replied. "I think the three of us need to have a little talk."

CHAPTER 26

Gramma came to the porch prepared in more ways than one. To begin with, she brought with her enough lemonade for all of us, but it soon became obvious that what she told us that evening was well-prepared, too. She had done her homework.

After we were all comfortable sitting on the porch I asked, "Gramma, what do you want to talk about?" She certainly had us curious. My initial thought was that she had caught us holding hands, and she was not comfortable with that. I should have known better.

"You two surely spend a lot of time in the woods," she replied as she ran her hands over her thighs brushing off invisible crumbs from her lap. "You remind me of your grandfather. He loved the woods so much." Gramma was a rocker; always in motion when she sat in a chair whether inside the house or outside where we were that night.

"Jake was the person who really got me into it," Netty said matter-of-factly. "Thanks to my dad, I have always loved nature, but I know a lot more now thanks to Jake. He shares stories about Grampa and lessons he learned from him about the forest."

Gramma smiled at Netty. There were times when I wondered just what Netty learned about me from Gramma when I was not around. The two could be thick as thieves one moment and very proper the next.

"Netty, my husband would have loved to have met you. From what I have noticed, he would have taken you out there with him along with this grandson of mine." She reached out and poked me saying, "He might even have left this guy behind!"

Shifting to a slightly more serious tone, Gramma continued to speak. "That's something I think we should discuss: your trips in the woods." Then Gramma looked squarely at me. "Jake McGee, you've been out there more than anybody. Just what is it you are looking for?"

Well there it was! No adult had ever asked me before whether or not I was looking for anything specific. A lump formed in my throat. I was wondering what she would think if I told her I was looking for Gramps, dead or alive.

"Aww, Gramma. I'm just a guy who likes the woods. Gramps taught me to appreciate it, and I do. I like to fish, I like to hunt, I–"

"Jake, I know all of that," she interrupted gently. "Let me back track a little. Let me ask you another question."

Netty looked at me, and I looked at her. Neither of us saw it coming. To say we were surprised by what we were about to hear is an understatement. When I think back on it, I know we were both flabbergasted, but relieved at the same time.

"Just how old do the two of you think I am?" She shook her finger and smiled saying, "Don't answer that!

"What I'm telling you both is that I've watched the two of you, and I think you're both up to something. And I love you for it, if you're doing what I *think* you're doing."

"Gramma, we're not–"

She put up both of her hands in front of me. "Let me finish." She took a breath and said, "I was up in the attic recently, too."

We both looked at each other immediately. She laughed softly at us.

"What? Do you think your old grandmother can't hike up those attic steps? Kids, I'm not 100 years old." She looked at me first and then to Netty, "Do I look like I'm 100?"

We both knew she was kidding, and Netty began to say, "Of course not, but–"

Again with the hands. Netty shushed.

"Your mom told me you were up there, and that's fine. I think it's nice that you were curious. I just wanted to find out why all of a sudden you were so curious about Grampa's things." Then she asked us the question that dictated the balance of that night's conversation. "Either of you rascals want to tell me about that?"

Silence. We heard Mr. Clemmons go by in his old truck. We waved. He honked. I did not know what Netty was thinking, but I was worried about upsetting Gramma if I told her the truth. Turns out she *knew* the truth.

"Okay. Let me tell you a little story first," she looked right at me and continued. "Did Netty ever hear about Gramps and the bank robbery?"

My head snapped up, and chuckled, "You're kidding. Right? Of course–"

"Yes, I've heard all about it!" Netty said excitedly. "Can you imagine what it was like to be there?"

"Netty, Dear, I *was* there."

My jaw dropped. "What did you say, Gramma?"

Despite the many versions I had heard over the years, I *never* knew Gramma was present when the robbery took place. She could tell I was surprised. This was a rabbit trail we wanted to follow.

"Yes, I was inside the bank. Why do you think Grampa was there?"

"I have always been told he was going through the drive-through window–"

"And he saw the look on Melissa's...what was her name?"

"Gardepe."

"Yes, Gardepe. He saw the look on her face, and that's what tipped him off." Gramma leaned forward as if to whisper something Top Secret. I'd rarely seen this storytelling side of her.

"But that's not what happened. You've grown up on that old man Jenkins's version, and you're brainwashed."

She smiled at the obvious disbelief on our faces. She knew she had us hooked. Gramma actually took her time. She drank some lemonade. I think she was savoring the chance to finally tell someone her version. Then I wondered why, if she had her own version, she had held it in all these years. As I was thinking about it, she nearly rocked me out of my seat when I heard what she said next.

"Ever hear his voice, Jake?"

"What?" I blurted out in disbelief.

"Does Grampa talk to you?" This time she waited...and waited. I was dumbfounded and said nothing in return. I gawked at Netty as if to ask, "I *just* told you about this. How did you ever get a chance to tell her?"

Netty looked at me knowing exactly what I was thinking and just shrugged her shoulders as if to say, "I'm as surprised as you are!"

Gramma's sage voice was heard to say, "Uh huh! Sometimes we say a lot when we don't say a word." She sat back in her rocker and said mysteriously, "Let me finish.

"Your grandfather drove me to the bank that day. I guess you could say we were in the "newlywed" stage of our lives. We did a lot of little things together that slip away later in many marriages. It's not a crime, but it's a shame it happens." More lemonade. Maybe she was thirsty from the storytelling, but I like to think she was milking the moment; enjoying her captured audience's attention.

"A gal likes it when a chair is pulled out, a car door is closed–"

"But Grampa did those things for you, Gramma. I saw–"

"Exactly, Jake." The look upon her face was happy and serene, as if she were going back in time to happier days. "Our life together was special. He was not the common man. It's one of the reasons I married him."

She sighed and took a breath. "But I'm forgetting the tale...my unabridged version of the story." She looked at Netty. "Where was I, Netty?"

"You were saying how you were inside the bank."

"Oh yes. I was. I was inside the bank when those two awful men came through the doors." Her look was distant as she recalled for us her tale. "They did have a hardened appearance. We could tell they meant business."

She paused as if for effect, but I don't think that is why she did it. I think it was just an emotional moment to share after so many years, making it tough for her to relive.

"That was the first time I ever spoke to your grandfather telepathically. Perhaps the emotion or fear wrapped up in the moment made it possible."

At this point, Gramma could have sprinkled in aliens from Mars. Nothing could have surprised us more. We were already off the charts when it came to surprises. Right in front of us on the porch was this woman, my grandmother who seemed to worry not one iota when we disappeared into the woods day after day, and now she was telling us she practiced telepathy.

"I told him, 'Jake Honey. I'm in trouble in here!' "

"Did he answer you?" I gasped.

"Yup. In a microsecond he asked me to sum up the problem, and I did. I don't mean to say we shared full sentences. It was as if I was sending mental pictures that he could somehow receive."

I had to ask. "Gramma, where did this whole *Mrs. Gardepe* version come from?" As soon as I asked, I hoped I did not hurt her feelings or sound as if I was doubting her.

"That's easy to explain. As your grandfather circled the bank to get into position, he drove right passed her. He actually did see the frightened look in her eyes and her standing there with her hands raised to her shoulders."

"So seeing her like that," added Netty, "confirmed what you had told him."

"Exactly and the rest of the story you've been told is pretty accurate."

"He actually pinned them against the bank wall?"

"Yes, that's exactly what your grandfather did. He was mad, too. Those two desperados are lucky he didn't push them through the bank wall and into the lobby."

As luck would have it, our little talk was suddenly forced to come to an end. Mom and Dad were pulling in with Netty's folks right behind them.

Calmly Gramma closed our conversation with, "We'll chat some more, you two."

Both of us countered simultaneously with, "When?" Gramma's trail had led us right back to where we started, sitting on the porch with questions begging for answers.

CHAPTER 27

As if scripted like a cliffhanger, our chat with Gramma was over. My parents unloaded groceries and invited the Carters into the house for a visit.

As they settled in, a conversation regarding the highway project unfolded. Mom and Mrs. Carter spoke of other people they met who were equally opposed. One of them was Attorney R.J. McGinnis out of nearby Hawley, nine miles down the road.

"Does he have a horse in this race?" Mr. Carter asked.

"Actually he does," Netty's mom shared. "He owns a twenty-acre parcel he purchased a few years back that also borders the game lands." She went on to explain that it was Mr. McGinnis's intention to someday retire upon the property, and like us he wanted no part of the increased annoyances a new highway would bring with it.

When the Carters said good night, Netty walked out with my grandmother. As Gramma watched from the porch, her eyes met those of my best friend. My grandmother signaled the universal "Call me" sign as she put her thumb and pinky finger to her ear. As she hopped into the Carter's dark green Jeep, Netty giggled and returned the gesture just before she shot a furtive glance in my direction. Their fun at my expense multiplied when they realized I had spotted their secretive gestures; their smiles making me wonder how often they really chatted with each other.

I took some teasing when Netty called later that evening. "What in the world would the two of you still have to discuss?" my dad asked with a wry smile as he looked across the room at my mom.

I'm not sure my grandmother was coming to my defense or she was siding with my folks. "Now I remember two other youngin's who spent a lot of time on the phone all hours of the day and night," Gramma interjected, sending my parents down Memory Lane. All three of them chuckled, and then I realized the implication of what she had said.

"Wait just a minute," I replied red-faced. "Gramma, are you saying what I think you're saying?"

Always a good actress, the surprised and innocent Gramma was the role she played as she replied, "Now Jake, just what *ever* are you talking about? I was just saying that I remember a time," she nodded toward Mom and Dad, "before these two lovebirds were married. It seemed like they were always on the phone."

Mom chimed in, too, with, "I had important matters to discuss with your son, Mrs. McGee. Surely you knew that!" My mother laughed lightly. All three of them were smiling. I felt my cheeks flush a deeper shade of red once I realized they really were hinting that Netty and I might be romantically involved.

There might have been an opportunity for the two of us to speak privately, but I knew Gramma wanted Netty to be present whenever we were to continue our conversation. To be honest, I felt the same way. How did I know she wanted it that way? She told me so, but it is how she told me that is worth sharing. This trail, albeit short, is important.

After the phone calls, after the teasing, and after some of Gramma's delicious Funny Cake Pie, a concoction that combines homemade vanilla cake, a base of rich chocolate syrup, and her prize-winning crust, I said good night and went up to bed. Not much later when all the house was still, I knew everyone had gone to bed, and our home had safely embraced us for the night.

It was dark and pretty quiet with the exception of August's katydid song being played by those rarely-seen, kelly green choir members. Then I thought I heard my grandfather say, "When the katydids sing, you can sleep, but when they don't, there's trouble deep." Grampa was full of natural lore, and some of it popped into my head from time to time.

But this time it wasn't *his* voice that popped into my mind. It was Gramma's! Not so much did I hear her voice, but I understood that the thoughts in my head were not my own or Grampa's but hers. What surprised me most was that I *was not* surprised!

Suddenly it all made sense. She had already told Netty and me she could connect telepathically with her husband, and that made me feel better about myself and the messages I had been experiencing. As a result, understanding thoughts transmitted by Gramma now seemed natural. I was receptive to it, so I guess my acceptance helped speed the process. What I did not know was how to reply, but I had to try. As an experiment, I requested Gramma make me her famous buttermilk waffles in the morning. I received no reply, but I swear I heard her laughing in her room next door to me.

What was important was that now I understood that Gramma wanted to continue our chat, but she wanted Netty present. I now understood that Netty was important to my grandmother, and that made me happy since Netty was my best friend.

As it turned out, we agonized for days over when we would next have enough private time with Gramma in order to continue our original conversation. We did not have to tell Gramma we were antsy. She, of course, *knew* we wanted to hear more of what she had to say on the matter of silent talents. At the same time, we knew we could not discuss it openly in front of my parents. Patience was the order of the day.

I was growing less patient by the day, but my cohort kept busy. Netty showed up at our house carrying two books. Enthusiastically she insisted I look at them immediately which I found odd until I saw what they were. One was *The Thought Readers* by Dima Zales and Anna Zaires. The second was by Eric Pepin entitled *Silent Awakening*. Always the better student, Netty had been doing some research on her own.

Up in my room we had begun discussing what Netty had learned by merely skimming through both books. "Some of it seems to stress that people can use their own mental energy to heal themselves," she told me. "What do you think?" she asked.

The whole concept was pretty foreign to me, but I was not going to argue. A new talent had exploded upon my life, and I had grandparents who practiced it, so I had to be open-minded, no pun intended.

"I remember reading a poster that impressed me with its message."

"What did it say?" Netty asked.

As best I could, I shared what I remembered. "The most dangerous phrase in any human language is, 'We have always done it this way.'" I could tell she did not understand, so I explained. "It means if folks are unwilling to try new things, we'll be stuck forever in one place. Maybe Gramma's on to something new; a different and better way of communicating."

A floorboard squeaked. "Well thank you, Jake," my grandmother said softly from the door to my room. Startled by her unexpected presence, we both jumped.

I gasped, "Gramma, you *have* to stop doing that! You're not here one minute, and then the next moment you're right behind us! You'll give one of us a heart attack!"

"Sorry, Kids. Listen," she went on to say, "your mother has gone to town. I came up here not to scare you, but to continue our talk from the other night when we were on the porch." I looked about my room and saw no place for the three of us to sit comfortably when she continued, "Let's go downstairs where we can all have a seat."

"Ok, Gramma. You—"

"Read his mind," Netty said with a laugh.

I looked first at Netty and then at Gramma who only smiled. "Oh no. Not you, too!"

Hearing Netty say, "Relax, Jake. It was a joke," did make me feel more at ease. "That was an easy one. Even I knew what you were about to say."

Gramma turned, and we followed her out of my room. The three of us made our way down the stairs into the living room. Gramma had her arm around my best friend's shoulder as she held on to the railing, too.

CHAPTER 28

Codger Menke decided he needed some time away from the courthouse. An avid golfer for several reasons, Codger especially liked the fact that he was able to choose who would be surrounding him for a couple of hours. On this day, he chose his grandson. To round out the foursome, Jeremy was permitted to bring along a pair of boys he knew from school. Much to Mr. Menke's surprise, he would learn that his grandson and the other boys showed some talent regarding the game of golf.

Menke chose to treat the boys by renting a pair of electric golf carts. "Jeremy and I will play against the two of you," Codger announced as they watched the group ahead of them plod their way up the first fairway. The day promised to be a beauty. Few members played in the afternoon, so it was quiet, plus the sky was the bluest of blues decorated with a few clouds which were the whitest of whites.

"Match play?" one of Jeremy's classmates asked as the boys stood in the tee box taking practice swings.

"Yes, Todd," Codger replied with a hint of surprise. "You know how to play like that?"

"Sure!" Todd went on. "Since we're playing in teams, our lower score will be matched against the lower score of your two balls after each hole."

"Okay then," Codger added. "What's the wager?"

Now it was the boys' turn to be surprised. Todd looked at his partner Mark, and then they both looked Jeremy who towered over them by at least six inches.

With a big smile, Jeremy eased his young opponents. "Relax, guys. Don't be wimps. Gramps just likes to play for a prize when he plays golf. We always compete for a soda. Losing team buys drinks from the machine for the winners. That's all."

Mark and Todd nodded. They both knew that they would have to agree to whatever stakes Jeremy announced, or they would never hear the end of it during school. Jeremy's guests loved golf, and they loved the course, but they also knew the only way they would have access to the club was if they tagged along with Mr. Menke or any other club member. Without a member invitation, the course was closed to the general public.

"You're our guests," Codger announced as he nodded up the first fairway. "Your team may tee off first, but watch out for the huge maple tree on the right and the traps on the left." Even in golf Codger Menke tried to gain an edge. His warning sounded like that of a guide, but he was really planting a seed of concern in the mind of each of his opponents.

He and Jeremy stood back and watched both young men rip their respective drives far up the middle of the fairway.

Oddly enough the trees were not a problem for young Todd or Mark, but proved to be a nuisance for both grandson and grandfather.

As they rode to their respective balls, Jeremy's grandfather spoke softly. "You didn't tell me these two were ringers, Boy."

Jeremy knew what his grandfather meant. He was reminding his grandson that he did not like to lose at anything to anyone. "Relax, Gramps. It's just the first hole of the day."

"Don't tell me to relax. The object is to get into *their* wallets, not the other way around."

Hole after hole, Codger pointed out the hazards facing his opponents. Hole after hole his warnings rattled them not in the least. Mark in particular proved to be a consistent adversary with his short game saving his team on a few of the first holes on the front nine. When he chipped in from twenty-five yards off the green to save a par, Todd and Mark hooted with glee and slapped high fives. Codger nearly had a kitten.

Observing his opponents' good fortune as he stood next to his grandson whose ball they discovered behind a small evergreen he uttered, "Looks like I picked the wrong partner, that's for sure." The comment hurt Jeremy more than a bit.

Walking off a two-tiered green after he missed a putt that would have tied the hole, Jeremy tried to express his issue with what his grandfather said to him. "Gramps, I know I'm not helping our score much so far, but we're not exactly playing for a million dollars."

"Jeremy, losers say things like that," Codger shot back. "No matter what we do, we do it to win. Now we're three down for God's sake."

They teed off on the next hole, a par three about 180 yards in length. Surprisingly Jeremy's tee shot was the best of the bunch. In fact, only his ball landed on the kidney-shaped green. Mark and Todd were on the fringe to the left while Codger was up to his neck in a pure white sand trap, also to the left.

As he sat in the golf cart, Jeremy needled his grandfather, giving him a taste of his own medicine. "Nice shot, Gramps. I hope *my* teammate can chip one in the hole."

He should have known better. Codger's retort stung him even more.

"I'll *have* to chip it in for us to have a chance. Lord knows you'll probably three-put from twenty feet."

Jeremy knew that most golfers, no matter how competitive they were, would have complimented him on his tee shot, especially if they were his partner. Even his opponents were complimentary, exhibiting good sportsmanship. It irritated Jeremy that his partner, his own grandfather, said the things he had said. He mulled it over and decided to clam up. They finished the front nine holes three holes down with nine to play, and all the boys went to the pro shop restroom while Codger slipped off to the clubhouse for a beer.

On their way back toward the tenth tee, Todd spoke to Jeremy.

"You're grandfather sure doesn't like to lose."

Mark added, "Yeah, Jer, we could hear a lot of what he said to you."

Not wanting to lose whatever social edge he had over these two boys, Jeremy scowled and said to both of them, "Mind your own business, and just play golf. This match ain't over yet." Deep down, part of him wished he had not spoken to them in that manner.

His comments made both boys wonder why they even hung out with Jeremy Teller at all, but in truth they both knew why. They were scared of him. It was Mark who spoke first when they knew Jeremy was out of earshot.

"The apple didn't fall from the tree. Did it?"

Todd quietly added, "Sour apple at that."

CHAPTER 29

On the back nine holes, Jeremy sickened of his grandfather's grumpy disposition, and he felt he needed to say something.

"Gramps, what makes you so tough and mean sometimes?"

Codger looked straight ahead. He was not about to apologize to his own grandson or anyone else. Instead, he chose to share a story.

"Boy, let me tell you something. See if you can follow where this brief verbal trail leads you." He began driving their cart a little slower. "Weakness and hesitation never gained anybody anything. I was raised to respect whoever is in charge, and as the result of my father's discipline I decided I wanted to *be* the person in charge."

Jeremy listened with greater-than-usual interest as his grandfather continued, for the man rarely spoke of his family.

"I have three brothers. All of them are older than I am. We grew up in a family that had solid rules that our father set down for all four of us." At this point in the tale, Codger had reached his ball, got out of their cart, and sized up his shot. He never once stopped talking.

"One of the biggest rules was meant to protect us from our own foolishness. We were raised to *never* cross the railroad tracks at the end of Grant Avenue which was where we lived as kids." Much to Jeremy's surprise, his non-stop, storytelling grandfather pulled off one terrific nine iron shot to the center of the thirteenth green.

"Those rails were the path of speeding commuter trains in and out Philadelphia, so being anywhere near them was dangerous." Codger stopped their cart by Jeremy's ball and waved for him to shoot. It was the only time he stopped talking during the telling of his tale. Jeremy, too, managed a decent shot to the green and hopped back onto their cart.

Codger Menke continued. "Crossing the railroad tracks had been done by my brothers before me. I knew that, but I also knew each of them had been punished for it."

This comment certainly caught Jeremy's interest, so he interrupted with, "What happened? How were they punished?"

"Our father owned a barber's strap. It was about two or three feet in length, and two inches wide. It was made of leather, of course."

Up went Jeremy's eyebrows. "He hit them with the strap?"

"Let me finish my story," Codger ordered, but Jeremy had to wait only momentarily as they finished putting on the green. They had even won the hole and were now only down one with three to play.

"Now what was I saying?" Codger asked even though he knew the answer to his own question.

"The strap! The punishment for your brothers crossing the tracks!"

Inwardly Jeremy's grandfather warmed. By his response, Codger knew he had his grandson's attention, and he decided that for effect he would finally slow down his delivery and make him wait some more. He nodded at the sixteenth's tee box.

"Tee up, Jeremy. We have the honors." To Todd and Mark he snorted, "Looks like this match might come down to the wire, boys." Then one more time he planted one of his famous seeds. "Watch out for the water on the right."

Jeremy once again landed his drive in primo position. How it was possible he knew not, but listening to his grandfather seemed to relax him. Codger, too, hit a fine drive albeit much shorter in distance than his grandson's. In their attempt to miss the aforementioned water on the right, Jeremy's guests drove their respective tee shots to the left and in the trees.

Once in the cart, Codger continued. "After we win this hole, we'll be in the catbird seat."

"Gramps!" Jeremy implored, "Tell the rest of your story."

"Oh...I forgot." No he didn't. "Let's see. Where was I?" he asked rhetorically. Before Jeremy could reply he continued.

"All through my youth my brothers would say to me, 'You never got the strap,' implying, of course, that they had received a beating to some degree at one point or another. They felt my father had mellowed over the years."

Codger went on to explain how one day when he was ten he was bullied into crossing the railroad tracks by an older neighborhood boy. Fifty plus years later he even still remembered the kid's name.

"Like you, Billy McGowan was bigger than his classmates. We feared him."

"Did he have friends?"

"Do you?" Codger shot back. It was a mean thing to say, but having a sharp tongue never seemed to bother Codger Menke.

Jeremy was stung by the comment but said nothing. His grandfather went on with his tale.

"Billy told me I had to follow him across the tracks. He'd found some tadpoles at a construction site." Codger went on to admit he had never seen real tadpoles before, so he was tempted to break the family rule anyway.

"McGowan wasn't asking me to go along. He was insisting, so I was going with him whether I liked it or not." Then he added, "The truth of the matter is that eventually I would have crossed those tracks on my own like my brothers had done before me. I wasn't much in favor of some of the rules my old man set."

As the story wound up and down, in and out, over and under, Jeremy learned the details of how his grandfather risked life and limb by crossing the railroad tracks where commuter trains raced by the Menke's neighborhood. As the tale played out, he also found out how as a boy young Richie ended up on the bully's homemade raft, the raft that took them to a clay dirt mound in the middle of a gigantic puddle where the tadpoles swam in the hundreds near the surface of murky, yellow-clay-colored water.

"I had to admit," said Codger, "that it really was a sight to see. However, when I turned around, Billy had taken off without me back to the edge of the puddle on his raft!"

"What did you do?"

"I panicked and jumped for the tail end of the raft. I accidentally sank it! There we both stood in two feet of water up to our knees in yellow clay. I knew right then my goose was cooked, and I was about to meet the strap."

Codger slowed down their golf cart as he watched the other lads hit their second shots poorly. The commissioner smiled knowing he and Jeremy were about to win the sixteenth hole as well.

"What happened next?"

Pretending to care, Codger whispered, "Jeremy, shush. I have to play my ball." With that Jeremy's grandfather once again tore into his Top Flite #4, landing it on the front of the green. The man seemed impervious to pressure.

When he approached to sit back down in the cart, Codger found Jeremy sitting behind the steering wheel. "Gramps, we're not budging from here until you finish your story."

Codger feigned resignation and put up his hands. "Ok. Those two will be a while anyway," he said as he nodded toward their young opponents.

"When I returned home, my mother knew where I had been."

"How? Had she seen you?"

"No. She just knew that the only clay in the area was at the construction site on the other side—"

"—of the tracks," Jeremy interrupted. "Go on."

"Well believe it or not," Codger went on to say, "there was a time in history when moms really did say the words, 'Wait until your father comes home!'"

"And?"

"So I was stripped of my filthy clothes, and I was sent to my room to wait." Codger watched Todd and Mark pick up their golf balls. They were conceding defeat on the sixteenth hole. The match was now all even with but two holes to play.

"What happened next?" Jeremy asked eagerly.

Nodding toward the seventeenth tee with the match all tied up, Codger said nothing.

"No. I meant what I said, Gramps. You have to finish the story before I move this cart."

His grandfather smiled. He had his grandson eating out of his hand.

"Okay. Okay." Codger sat quietly for a brief spell as if struggling to recall that day so long ago. In reality, he was milking the moment, pausing again for effect, a skill he used on the campaign trail. Then he continued.

"For a few minutes, I heard nothing but my mother in the laundry room cleaning my clothes. Then I heard something I've never forgotten." Codger put his arm around his grandson. "Through my bedroom door I heard my oldest brother tell my other brothers, 'Richie's gonna get the strap!'" Menke went on to say he actually heard his brothers begin a chant.

" 'He's gonna get the strap! He's gonna get the strap!' until our mother chased them out of the hallway outside my bedroom door."

"Eventually my father did come home, and I guess you know what happened after that."

"Really? You're dad whipped you with a barber's strap?" Living in a world now when such occurrences were labeled child abuse, such as the time when football superstar Adrian Peterson was taken to court for using a thin tree branch to chastise his own son, Jeremy could hardly believe what he was hearing.

"You bet he did," Codger grunted. "You didn't mess with our old man. He ruled the roost. He was tough."

"Geez!" Jeremy exclaimed.

The older man snapped his head toward his grandson; fire in his eyes. "What's *that* supposed to mean, Jeremy? My father's strap helped make me the man I am today."

Eyes wide open, Jeremy wanted to ask his grandfather if he even knew what people in town thought of him, the man he was today. Jeremy heard what people said about Codger Menke. Yet the man was a walking enigma. If folks did not like him, then why was he elected Commissioner?

"Did he yell at you a lot?"

Codger replied more calmly, "Oh things like, 'Are you ever going to cross the tracks again?'"

"That's it?" Jeremy asked one more time to be sure he was understanding this tale correctly. He was beginning to understand, perhaps, why his grandfather was the person he was. Jeremy thought it might also explain why his own mother was so quiet all the time. He had to wonder whether or not his grandfather treated his own daughter in a similar fashion.

"Are you kidding?" Grampa put a finger in Jeremy's chest. "He rode us hard, but we all turned out to be successful. Tough discipline didn't kill us.

"He proved he was still in charge every time he smacked us. He was tough, but we learned to respect rules." Codger's chin jutted out, and finished speaking. "I decided then and there that when I grew up I wanted to be like him." Codger nodded toward Mark and his partner on the next tee as he said, "Your friends are waiting. Let's go finish 'em off."

CHAPTER 30

Gramma invited us to sit as she brought us a cold drink and a snack, just like she always did. We were in the kitchen, a bright, cheerful place with its white cabinets and honed, black marble countertop. In our home, the kitchen was our headquarters. She always said it was her favorite room in the house.

Finally she joined us at our table. As grandmothers seem to go, mine was a pretty woman who cared about her appearance. She did not hide her gray hair, but on her it looked like silver and appeared regal. No one ever saw her with her hair a mess. Like most days, she was wearing nice jeans, and she wore a pretty pink top.

She wasted no time picking up where we left off. Wrapping her fingers around her own cold drink, she spoke to us.

"Okay, you two. It's been a few days, so let's continue with any questions you might have." She sipped her iced tea. It was homemade. She taught me how she would boil water in our teapot. Our teapot was designed to look like a white rooster with a red comb and black beak. Its beak matched the handle across the top of the pot. Into the boiled water she would slip five tea bags to steep along with five sprigs of fresh mint from our garden. After an hour it was ready to be diluted to whatever strength was needed. Gramma's iced tea was the best.

Netty began to speak for both of us. "Mrs. McGee—"

"Netty, I've heard you refer to my husband as 'Grampa', and I like it. Please call me 'Gramma'. Okay?" She smiled at her new granddaughter.

"Really? Okay," Netty said a little red-faced. I could tell she was ecstatic. One of her grandmothers had already passed away. Gramma helped fill a void. After a deep breath, Netty started again.

"Gramma," she said softly while pausing to enjoy how it felt to her, "did you have connections with any of your other family members?"

"No," my grandmother replied. "None that I recall." Then she looked at me and teased, "But I did have a dog who seemed to read my mind."

"That's not funny, Gramma," I replied. "That's just weird." Netty and Gramma giggled.

"I'm sorry," she said. "I couldn't resist it. Besides, some day you might be having this same conversation with your own grandchild. You might find it goes best if you keep the conversation lighthearted, Jacob."

"Yes, Ma'am." Then I thought of *my* question. "The other night you shared with me Grampa's old saying about katydids. I knew it was you, but I wasn't sure how to return a message or thought to you."

With a *big* smile on her face she countered, "So you asked for my buttermilk waffles."

I nearly flipped. By the look on my face, Netty realized the degree of my surprise.

"Gramma! Why didn't you tell me you—"

"What?" interrupted Netty. "What happened? Where was I?"

I explained to Netty how a few nights earlier my grandmother and I had our first telepathic connection; shared our thoughts for the first time.

"Whoa! *That is way cool!*" was her reaction.

Netty was special and full of her own kind of surprises. I must have expected her to register some degree of disbelief about all of this. I guess I even expected a level or degree of envy or jealousy. Instead, she was as supportive as ever, just like the day in the woods when I brought her into all of this. She was the least judgmental person I had ever met.

I looked at her and simply said, "It was. It really was." Then I had a private, silent thought of my own. I wondered when Netty had become so pretty.

"She's always been that way," Gramma said to me aloud after another sip of tea. "You just hadn't noticed until now."

"What?" asked Netty. "What did you say, Gramma?"

I just stared at my grandmother. She *knew* what I had just been thinking. For a second I lost my breath. Would I never again have a private thought? And would she now report to my best friend what I had been thinking?

Gramma looked at Netty. "This young man right here..."

Oh boy! Here it was!

"...was just thinking how much he appreciates your support."

Netty turned to me and said, "Sure. We're best buds." Then suddenly she realized what just had taken place. She understood that Gramma had just read my mind. That begged the next question.

As she asked it she pointed at me. "Gramma, will you always be able to know what this guy is thinking?" We both eagerly awaited the answer.

My grandmother played the moment like a fiddle. I suspect she performed on stage in her younger days, for she surely knew how to capture an audience.

"No, Netty. I can't do that," Gramma finally announced.

I sighed a breath of relief loud enough to be heard and understood. Netty giggled again at my expense in a friendly manner.

From there Gramma went on to share memories about a few other times when she and her husband connected in their secret silence. I was proud to learn their talents were never used against anyone else or for any kind of gain regarding themselves.

She told of a time when Gramps went for one of his hikes off of McGee land and into the State Game Lands.

"I guess some days he knew I was wondering where he was and whether or not he was okay. At times like that he'd somehow let me know he was fine." Then she added, "Once in a while he'd share what he was seeing if it was special to him."

"You understood details?" I asked.

"Rarely. It was more like a snapshot of a scene, I guess."

"But once in a while you did perceive details?" I repeated.

"I'm not so sure," she said. Then as if she was suddenly surprised and saddened at the same time she recalled, "In fact, the very day your grandfather went away I thought he told me about a stone bridge far out among the trees. I just knew that couldn't be right. That and something about an extraordinary rabbit."

CHAPTER 31

Not many days of the final two weeks before school went by
without the three of us exploring more of the State Game
Lands, yet it was to no avail. We were never able to find the
stone bridge a second time, nor did we come across any hint
of my grandfather ever having been there. And the rabbit?
Forget the rabbit. Certainly Artie would have discovered its
trail again if it had been anywhere near us.

The last weekend of vacation revealed summer at its best,
and we were out and about until late afternoon. "It has to be
here," I whooshed out of my mouth as I sat down for a rest.
The cool drink from my canteen was refreshing. "If we saw it,
and if Grampa saw it, it has to be here someplace."

Netty was directly under an evergreen tree resting atop a
bed of golden-brown needles. Thin patches of sunlight flit-
tered around her on the ground.

"And according to Gramma, he did indeed see it," and
then she added with a hint of a hopeful tone, "so we know he
was here."

"How could a stone bridge just disappear?" I mumbled.

"Come on," she said. "It's time we get back to the house."

I looked all around. Golden sunlight beamed down through the branches when it could make its way to a path, and painted the groundcover in its deepest greens. Pathways were narrow, but where they could be seen the sunlight gave them a rich, deep-brown appearance accented by the occasional rocks that emerged through the surface.

I pointed downward toward a path ahead. "Toe breakers. That's what Grampa called those gray rocks, the ones that stick up along the path."

"He's right. And I can't believe we've not fallen over any of them at least once while we've been out here."

I looked at her and said, "Careful, Netty. Don't jinx us."

"Jake, can you imagine what it would be like to be hurt out here if you were by yourself?" She thought a moment. "It would be bad enough if we were together." Quickly she became insistent. "*Promise* me you won't come out here alone ever again," she requested, beseeching me to acquiesce. I knew she was asking because she was concerned, and I appreciated it.

I tossed one of the million rocks I had tossed over the years and said, "What do you mean?"

"Let's pretend one of us tripped over a toe breaker and broke something else as well. What should we do?"

She was right. We had never before discussed such a possibility.

"Depending on the injury," I finally suggested, "one of us might have to go for help. Artie would stay behind for company—"

"And protection?" she asked with more than a little dis-comfort in her voice.

I surprised myself with my answer. "Yes, and for protec-tion." It just felt strange to be worried all of a sudden after all the times I had been in the forest and had never given safety a thought.

"Well I guess there is another option," my colleague in exploration (my mother's words, not mine) began to explain. "There's always the chance that Gramma would know some-thing was wrong, too."

"Yeah, but sometimes...almost all the time...messages are not exchanged in details or specifics." I didn't like admit-ting that. "Gramma told us that. Right?"

"Yes, but at least it's something. It's a possibility."

As we continued our walk home with Artie on a lengthy rope leash, we continued to discuss the possibility of emergencies.

"We've agreed with Gramma," offered Netty, "that we shouldn't tell our parents what we've been doing, and tell-ing them about our mental connection is *definitely* out of the question."

I ducked under a thick, low-hanging maple tree branch. She followed. For a while both of us were quiet, so quiet that once again the forest birds were seemingly noisy. Crows, car-dinals, and even blue jays flitted about as if talking to each other. Not too far off to our right, a large pileated wood-pecker worked for insects in an old deciduous tree. Its body was beautifully accented in the afternoon sunlight; largely black with a brilliant, fluffy, red crest while its throat and neck were largely white. Its hollow-sounding *knock knock knock knock-ing* boomed throughout the trees.

I finally broke our silence. "Netty, maybe we *should* tell our parents a little something, just so they know where we are."

"Yeah, but how much?"

"How much what?"

She touched my arm gently as if to stop me. Again I noticed immediately that I liked it. Somehow her touch made our bond seem stronger, and I wondered if she felt that way, too.

"How much should we tell them?"

"Well," I thought, "we can tell them where we'll be exploring."

"And anything else?"

I gazed over her shoulder at where we had been that day. Suddenly the forest seemed bigger to me; more ominous. I did not like how that made me feel.

"Maybe we should give them a definite time to expect us home."

"We already do that pretty much," she countered.

"But if we were specific," I said as I looked at her, "it would make everyone a bit more attentive. You know what I mean?"

"Yes," she said as she tilted her head, "I guess so. They'd be more aware of our arrival time and would come looking if we were late. And we'd be more careful about getting back on time."

"Exactly."

We eventually stopped at the stone wall marking the beginning of McGee land. Both of us were a bit uneasy. We had never thought about the dangers of the forest before which was odd considering Grampa seemingly disappeared there.

"We can't tell them why we're exploring so often?" she tossed out.

"Oh God no!" I was surprised she even asked. "They'd make me stop looking."

"Okay. Should we tell them about the bridge at least?"

I was curious about her line of thinking. "What are you getting at?"

"Well, they might be curious enough to come looking with us at least once, and who knows what any of us might find?" She suspected I was not clearly following her reasoning, so she reworded her point. "Do you care who finds anything when it comes to Grandpa, Jake, or just that answers are found?"

I was pleasantly surprised. "I never thought of it like that. I guess we *could* get them out here looking for the bridge. Couldn't we? The more eyes the better."

CHAPTER 32

Labor Day weekend whistled through our lives like an old steam engine that used to chug along the line through town. We were back in school, and we were the upper classmen of the building. Top dogs. There were several things that made eighth grade special. When our students reached the eighth grade, all of us could take part in autumn's traditional trip to the theater in October and Red Ribbon Week later the same month. Not until eighth grade were students eligible to play in the Turkey Tip Off as a reward for citizenship. Each year our annual Faculty vs. Students basketball game was the November highlight that ended our traditional food drive and began our Thanksgiving vacation. Similarly no one but the school's eighth grade class has ever been permitted to attend the middle school's Dress Up Dance in the spring. The Dance is like a rite of growing up; eighth graders dress like adults and are treated as such when the cafeteria is transformed into a magical nightclub-like setting. For these reasons alone, everyone was excited to be in a eighth grade.

Well…most of us. Like in schools everywhere, there's a slice of the student population that could find problems with puppies, ice cream, and cash handouts. I fully expected one such group to be comprised of my old nemesis Jeremy Teller and his boys. I kept my distance, but it was difficult not to see him. Jeremy was as tall or taller than most of the teachers in our school. Sad to say, he brought with him a history of tormenting and browbeating others. Yet despite his being a jerk, I felt bad for him.

"Being Codger Menke's grandkid can't be easy," my dad said on more than one occasion. "When you can, give the kid some slack. It might pay off."

Eighth grade presented yet another test for me. Netty was in very few of my classes. When we compared our schedules at lunch the first day of school, I found myself hoping she was as disappointed as I.

"At least we're in Study Hall together each day," she pointed out. "And look! We have Home Ec together!"

"That's just dandy," was my witty response to that discovery. "We can have a cooking contest on weekends." Inside I was smiling. At least we had a few classes together in school.

Then I remembered. "Wait! That means we will have Shop and Art Class together as well. Home Ec is only for one marking period."

"I don't mind the artsy part," she groaned, "but Shop Class?"

"C'mon, Netty," I teased. "I'll show you how to build a better bird house." She acted as if the thought was not very funny, but then she laughed.

Lunch in the cafeteria had always been and will always be an accurate cross section of social behaviors and cliques. From Day Number One of any school year, friends have sought out friends in the cafeteria. Jocks sit with jocks, and musicians sit together as do all the kids who worry about the labels on their clothes. They are referred to as "Preps" or "Preppies". Then there is the slice of the cafeteria pie that everyone avoids: bullies. We all knew who sat at their table.

After we were all given the Riot Act and told by our principal how eighth graders were to set an example for underclassmen, the teachers on Lunch Duty finally let us line up to get our lunches. Some kids still brought their lunches with them, so they hustled up front, bought their milk or ice cream, and sat down, hoping they would go unnoticed. For some reason, maybe because they were jealous, each year a handful of tormentors called out and poked fun at the "baggers".

"What's the matter?" they would yell. "Can't your parents afford to buy you a lunch?" Those jerks knew the teachers would squelch their loud calls with a hard-lined threat of detention even on the first day of school, but in yelling at least one time they felt they had achieved some sort of sick social victory by simply labeling the baggers for another year. Me? I admired the baggers. In fact, I was one of them. We had the best lunches in the cafeteria.

Some days Netty bought lunch, and some days she was a bagger, too.

Either way, we sat together among our friends and enjoyed lunch as best we could.

And loud? Oh it was loud in the cafeteria! Teachers actually wore protection in their ears since they never figured out a way to permanently quiet students down. After all, lunch time was our social time as well as our time to gulp down some goodies. Nothing like a good, balanced lunch of pop, snacks, and candy to prep all of us for afternoon classes. I bet classroom teachers loved their classroom period immediately following lunch.

Know what else happens in an eighth grade lunch? Tough guys *look* for victims, and few things draw much more attention than boys and girls sitting together. Those of us who sit with members of the opposite sex might as well wear a bull's-eye on our backs. No matter how loud our cafeteria might be, it seems bullies have the loudest voices ever designed just to command the attention of everyone while announcing what brought them delight. Boys sitting with girls were a natural target, and bullies seldom miss their mark.

The odd part? I never once saw male bullies sit with any female bullies. It just did not happen. At least they were philosophically consistent with each other. That meant that when one section made an announcement about their intended victims, it was almost immediately echoed by bullies of the opposite sex. Twice the fun!

After a curious look around at the lay of the land, I noticed something that first day of eighth grade, and above the din of all that was going on, I mentioned it to Netty. "Where's Teller?"

"What?" she yelled back even though we were seated across from each other.

"Where is Jeremy Teller?" Then I added, "He *can't be* suspended already!"

She looked. We looked. A whole bunch of us looked. When we found him, we were semi-shocked. He was where we expected him to be: among the thugs. What we did *not* expect was that he was being quiet, and we all knew that a quiet intimidator could be a scary thing.

CHAPTER 33

School was going well, and summer slipped into autumn. Even before I was a teen, I liked fall weather and how leaves changed colors. However, I never did like to rake leaves and bag them. Dad asked me to do it, and I did it, but I never liked it.

Strangely enough, on the second Saturday in October I found myself raking leaves at the home of one of my friends from school, Medhat Labib. At his request, at school he was nicknamed "Matt". His father was killed in a tragic accident a few years before I met him during seventh grade. Looking for a fresh start, they moved to Honesdale where he lived alone with his mom. I remember thinking how life would be for me if I ever lost my dad. Then, of course, my father was a guy who already lost his own dad at a pretty young age. When Gramps disappeared, my father was only thirty-seven.

I liked Matt, and one day during school I invited him out to our place. I had already cleared it with my parents. I told them about him and how he was in a single-parent situation. They were fine with me having him over to our home.

"Thanks, Jake, but I promised my mom I'd rake leaves this weekend." He didn't say it, but I suspected that for an instant he was wishing his dad was around to help; something a son might do with his dad each fall like shooting hoops or tossing a football. I figured he just *had* to miss time with his father. I know I would if I had been in his situation.

When I asked, "Do you want some help?" I saw his demeanor change instantly.

"Really? You'd do that with me?"

"Sure. We'll get it done more quickly that way. Then we can do whatever."

Matt lived in town almost directly across the street from our school. He nodded and happily said, "Ok!" Then a bit more excitedly he added, "If we have time left over we can go shoot some hoops." He nodded toward our school. Matt excelled at basketball, but I did not. That didn't matter to him. He just liked to play, and I just thought that the two of us hanging out together would be fun no matter what we did.

So there I was on a Saturday in early October raking leaves at somebody else's house. It was incredible outside. Autumn sky gets no more blue and the temperature was perfect. For some reason, raking leaves was an easier pill to swallow when I was helping a friend do it. As I did the work, I realized that there is something special about the sound of metal rakes dragging across turf; unique to autumn, especially when it scratches over a sidewalk or blacktopped driveway. If I were blindfolded and heard the sound, I would know exactly what it was.

We were not meticulous about the yard work, but we did a decent job. We were almost done by one o'clock. His mom thanked us and tossed a couple of burgers on her grill.

Once we had eaten, we hurried back outside to finish. His yard was tilted slightly downhill toward the road, so it seemed only natural to rake leaves in that direction and bag them down at the street's edge. As we were winding up the task, along came Jeremy Teller with another guy. I recognized the other boy from school, but I did not know his name since I did not hang out with the likes of Jeremy.

"Matt," I whispered, "just keep raking. Don't say anything." My friend and I were both hoping they would just pass by without incident. They didn't.

"Don't see you in town too much, Jake," Jeremy said as he walked by. "Watcha doin'?"

My first thought was that he would have to be a moron to not realize what we were doing, but I reconsidered telling him so, and I just nodded to my left and uttered, "Helping out Matt."

"Hey, Teller. Hey, Phil," Matt said softly. Evidently he knew the other kid. "When we're done we're gonna go shoot some hoops at the school."

I cringed. I found myself wishing he never told Jeremy that part. Then came the surprise of the day.

"Really?" Teller tossed back. "Maybe we'll see you over there."

That wasn't the part that surprised me. I was surprised when he asked, "Would you mind if we joined you?" Since when did Teller ask anybody's permission to do anything?

"Sure. We'll see you around," Matt said coolly.

Phil said not one word the entire time. I found that to be a bit odd, but I realized he probably didn't know me either. I wondered to myself how well Matt knew Jeremy, so I decided to ask.

"You know those two very well at all?"

Matt stopped raking, and looked at me. "Doesn't everyone?"

"So you know what Teller can be like?" I wanted to know how much Medhat Labib knew about the biggest bully in the school.

"I've heard some things," he admitted. "But he's never bothered me personally."

"Lucky you," I countered. Then I remembered my dad's advice and shrugged. "Who knows? Maybe he's changed."

With a big smile on his face, Matt looked at me and started to laugh.

"Who knows, Jake," he said humorously as he seemed to be studying the prongs on his rake, "maybe he's…turned over a new leaf!" After I ran him down, that's when we started wrestling. Woodsman that I was, I wrestled like Matt played basketball. He didn't stand a chance.

CHAPTER 34

On Sunday morning, the day after I helped Matt with his yard work, Mr. Carter, my parents, Netty and I were finally off exploring the State Game Lands next to our property. I was walking next to Netty and telling her about my day with Matt and how Jeremy came along. I revisited the entire scenario.

"It's odd," she said when she knew I was finished, "that he politely asked if he could join the two of you. I find it even more odd that he didn't show up, especially after making a point of being polite."

I helped her over the stone wall at the edge of our property. That was something new to our routine, and I liked it despite the fact that we both knew she no more needed my help than our fathers did.

"Yeah," I added, "that's the funny thing. Why would he behave so out-of-character and then not show up? I gotta tell ya. I was leery when he asked." We walked into the shade of the trees at the forest's edge. "I am now even more leery since he didn't show. I am wondering if it was some sort of set up."

Just then my father called to us, "Which way?"

This particular Sunday outing was the long-overdue result of our finally confiding in our parents. As agreed, we did not tell them everything we could have told them, but just enough to get them to come along. As Netty said, "It will be nice to have extra sets of eyes."

About a month earlier, just after school had started and everyone had once again adjusted to our new routine, Gramma, Netty, and I agreed it was time to approach our folks.

"I think you're wise," she said, "in making this decision. At some point, they might have asked that you not go into the woods so often now that autumn is here."

"Why might they do that?" I inquired. "We've done it so many times before."

"I don't know. Call it a hunch."

Netty summarized our plan one more time. "We agree to tell them about the bridge."

"And the rabbit?" I interjected.

"Yes. Even the rabbit. Remember that partially explains Artie's behavior that day."

My grandmother added, "And don't forget to mention you'll be telling them when and where you plan to go; when you'll be returning."

"Right," we both replied simultaneously.

The day we finally opened up to our parents, the Carters had been over for a picnic, so the timing felt right. As planned, Gramma brought up the highway project once again and how it might jeopardize some of the State Game Lands. We saw our chance and took it once the adult portion of the conversation had played out.

I was clumsy. I fumbled with my words. Netty waited patiently. Perhaps because we were at my house, and perhaps because all the exploration was originally meant to satisfy me, she let me do the talking.

"Netty and I saw a couple of things in the woods we would like to tell you about," I finally was able to express. "It was quite a while ago. Artie was with us, and he ran us ragged."

Our parents chuckled at my facial expression when I emphasized Artie's role. Just as quickly they quieted; interested in hearing the rest of our story.

"What did you see, Jake?" Mom asked.

"This is going to sound really strange, but believe it or not we came across an arched bridge made of field stone; just one arch. That's all it was."

"What ran under it?" Mr. Carter wanted to know.

Netty spoke up. "That's just it, Dad. There was nothing under it. There was no reason for a bridge to even be there. At least that was how it looked to us."

"Maybe at one time there was a stream that ran through that part of the woods," he replied. "Did the bridge look old? Perhaps over the years things just dried up."

"Mr. Carter," I responded to his idea, "we stood back and looked for some sign of a slope or gully that might have directed water under it. We didn't see a thing."

During the entire time we bounced possible explanations back and forth, Gramma was quiet. No one found that odd, so it went unnoticed for a bit. After that part of our discussion played out, my father asked the big question.

"Can you show it to us?"

By the tone of his voice, I knew he wasn't doubting us. He was not questioning our sincerity. He just wanted to know if they could see it.

"Well that's the weird part, Dad." I paused. I scratched my head, and I took a glimpse at Netty.

"We haven't seen it since!" she finally blurted out. "We've looked several times and retraced our steps from that day. We even took Artie along hoping he would lead us there again."

"What do you mean?" Mrs. Carter asked.

I looked at Netty's mom and told her. "Actually it was Artie who found it first." I went on to explain again how he was all over the forest that day. I told of how Netty and I took turns running full out just to keep up. I even told them that we suspected he was on the trail of a rabbit when he found the bridge.

"Ok," my dad said. "Let me see if I am following you correctly. The three of you went in the forest. Artie got onto a rabbit trail. The trail led you all over God's creation, because that's what rabbits do, and you eventually came to a small, stone bridge in the middle of the woods where there was no trace of a stream ever having been there." He looked at both of us. "Do I understand you correctly?"

We nodded. For a bit of time there was an uncomfortable quiet. I guess we should not have been surprised at what was said next, but we were pleasantly surprised indeed.

Netty's father looked at my father and each of their wives and said, "Well, I guess we're going to have to help you find the bridge."

"Really, Dad?" Netty cried out. "You believe us?"

"Why would we not believe you?" he countered. "You're our kids."

Then Gramma dropped the bomb shell. All during this conversation my mom and Mrs. Carter had spoken very little. But Gramma? She had not said a single word. When she finally spoke she seemed to magically take the air from the room.

"Dan, once long ago your father saw the bridge, too." She said it so matter-of-factly that there seemed to be no doubt that Gramps had seen it. "He never found it again either."

"Mom," my father asked as he revealed a tad of surprise, "when did he tell you that?"

"It was long ago. You were not much older than Jake is today." When spoken out loud like that, the whole idea just sounded so mysterious.

"He never told me about it," my dad replied. "I wonder why." Again, my dad's words were expressed in such a manner that we all knew he was not questioning the veracity of Gramma's words. Perhaps he felt left out of the loop.

Since bombs were dropping, I guess Netty thought she would drop another. I had alluded to it earlier, but now it was time to tell the rest of the story.

"There's more," she announced. "Remember the rabbit Jake mentioned? The one we think Artie was after?" She did not give our parents time to respond. "Well, it was the biggest rabbit either of us have ever seen, and we've not seen it since that day either."

"Maybe it wasn't a rabbit," Mr. Carter offered.

"Maybe it was a coyote," my mother said a second later. "Lots of them are roaming about."

I spoke up and said, "No. It was definitely a rabbit, but it was huge."

My dad actually laughed and lightened the mood. "All right," he said chuckling. "It looks like we're going rabbit hunting...down by the ol' bridge." We laughed about it, but we wondered about it, too.

And that was how Sunday in the Game Lands came about. Our exploration did not take place as soon as we would have liked, but at least it was happening. Nearly a month had passed since that night, and the topic came up more than a few times. The problem was finding a day when everyone was free. Finally this particular Sunday, the second Sunday of October was the day, and even then Mrs. Carter could not arrange to be there.

All of us were looking for a bridge, "...the biggest rabbit known to man..." as my dad would say, and Netty and I were still looking for Grampa.

To our disappointment, during that exploration with our parents we discovered nothing we had not discovered on our own. Mr. Carter and my parents understood our feelings, and he offered two suggestions.

"First of all, kids, we can look some more on another day. But I think it might be a good idea," he continued, "to speak to an officer who works for the Game Commission between now and then. Let's find out what they might have to offer on the subject."

"Who knows what we'll find with the help of a professional," Mom offered. I'm sure she was trying to give us some hope.

CHAPTER 35

The following week in school witnessed the return of the Jeremy Teller we all had grown to "know and love" as we put it. On Monday, he loudly dubbed our table the "co-eds". Of course, his action earned the ever-popular double guffaw from the male and female bully tables. Up until then, at least, he had been pretty subdued in the cafeteria. He did trip a preppy once, and that was always good for a laugh among the school bullies at someone else's expense. That day he was given a lunch detention which meant he ate alone where everyone could see him. Our table was positive he enjoyed being seen alone. Call it free advertising.

I can only imagine that under normal circumstances most middle school kids show no interest in local elections. Our social studies teachers had been trying to emphasize the importance of voting on local and state issues, but to no avail. It took Jeremy Teller to stir up interest. I think it began during his lunch detention. I think he planned the whole thing.

Codger Menke's term as Wayne County Commissioner was nearly at an end, and he had a lot to lose. If he was not

"Commissioner Menke" in the spring, Crown Developers would have no further interest in him. A lot of money would be lost, money that Jeremy's grandfather coveted.

Up for reelection in November, Mr. Menke was smart enough to realize that if he leaned on his grandson he might squeeze a few votes out of the classmates' parents. During late August, Codger had begun organizing an *Adopt a Highway* program that would run right by the school's entrance, and he would be its sole sponsor. For three months, the name "Richard Menke" and his good intentions would be posted for every voting parent to see when driving by the school, advertised in easy-to-read, white letters upon one of those popular royal blue signs.

It just so happened that the same week Jeremy had earned his lunch detention, he not only wore a large "Vote for Menke" button all day, but he and his posse also began cornering kids in the hallway between classes.

"Hey!" he informed most eighth graders while teachers were not close by, "I want to see you at the cleanup project Saturday morning." His buddies casually circled Jeremy's recruits so teachers were unable to see him in action. I have to give him credit. Teller was always careful not to tell kids what might happen if they did not show up. No one could accuse him of issuing threats.

I knew it would happen eventually, so when he approached me on the subject I was ready. He was a bit taken back by my approach.

"Teller," I said loudly enough for kids nearby to hear as he lumbered towards me, "I hope I see you at the *Adopt a Highway* project Saturday morning!" Then I added frosting to the proverbial cake. "Do you want my dad and me to pick you up?"

He did not like it one bit, but what could he do? Peer pressure is a double-edged blade.

My parents were pretty pleased when I told them how I handled the whole Jeremy-comes-a-recruiting event. My father asked me about Jeremy's response.

"What did he say?" Dad asked.

"There wasn't much he could say without being threatening. He just sort of grunted and looked around menacingly at the few kids in the hall who heard me say it."

My dad made a good point. "I bet he was coached."

"Coached?" I asked.

"Sure. I bet his grandfather drilled into him just exactly what *not* to do." Then he added, "Remember, Codger needs votes not enemies. That's the only reason he organized this project on Saturday."

Mom sat down with us at the table. We were enjoying a dessert she made with Gramma, a layered chocolate cake with peanut butter frosting.

As she sliced the cake and handed me my piece she said to me, "Jake, you do realize now that you *have* to show up Saturday."

Gramma added, "If you don't show up you will have lost any credibility you have with this Teller lad."

"What do you mean?" I asked my grandmother and my mother.

"Well," she said, "it sounds to us like you cleverly served a dessert of your own. It's called Humble Pie."

"What?" I was confused.

Mom took over. "Jake, you were probably the first person to put this boy in his place, and you did it in front of classmates. If you don't help out on Saturday, you will have become just like him."

I thought about what they said, and I realized they were right. I did it to myself again. I'd be raking all over again! Same street...different cause.

"I guess I'll call Medhat Labib," I told my folks. "He loves raking almost as much as I do." We had a good laugh, some terrific cake, and later I called Netty to see if I could con her into coming along.

CHAPTER 36

Netty Carter showed up. I knew she would, and I'm glad she was there to see what happened later that day.

After my little public speaking stint in the eighth grade hallway for the benefit of one Mr. Jeremy Teller, he pretty much left me alone the rest of the week. I kept waiting for the other shoe to drop, but it never did. I guess that in his own way, Jeremy's choice to not come back at me was as effective in messing with my own mind as if he had done something to me. I just would never admit that to him. And to be honest, when I told Netty what I was thinking I had to agree with her when she said, "I don't think Jeremy Teller's smart enough to do that to you."

Yet I have to give credit to Jeremy. Of course, I did not condone his methods, but at least fifty kids showed up. I did not count them, but there was a mob, and I have to say, too, that various cliques were represented. Jeremy was definitely an equal opportunity bully.

Pictures were taken for the local paper. Right in front of everyone stood Codger Menke and his grandson. We were all positioned in front of the now-famous blue and white sign for what my father later called the "Three P's" or "primo propaganda positioning."

After the photo opp, Mr. Menke took off without saying a word to any of us; not a "Thank you", not a wave, not even a honk of his horn. He simply handed the reporter a press release and hopped in his car. I do not think he cared at all that we were there.

Codger must have made some campaign promises, for there were adult volunteers there to instruct us and to help make sure we were safe. Along the two-mile stretch of road that ran passed our school, there were police officers who sat in their cars with their lights flashing at each end of the event as well as one in the middle. That was a nice touch. Kids joked about seeing donuts exchanging hands when the Commissioner showed up.

Nearly everyone brought gloves to protect their hands, and white plastic bags were randomly distributed. Anything too large for bagging was simply put in community piles along the roadside. Some of what we collected were tires, aluminum cans, plastic bottles, a lawn mower, and even a suitcase. At that, a mom stepped in and warned that the suitcase probably should be opened by someone in charge. "We might not want to know or smell what's inside of that," she said. It turned out to be nothing special.

I saw Teller and some of his friends helping out, but never once did we speak. I was certain he saw me, for when our eyes met I waved. Again I expected some sort of retaliation, but nothing happened, not even an unfriendly glare.

By the time we finished, the township trucks arrived to pick up all that was collected, and it was up to them to dispose of everything. The entire stretch of road looked great.

Walking back toward the school, I had a moment to speak to Netty about what we had just done. She had been cleaning along the road with some girls she knew.

"Look at us," I joked. "Think we'll be sitting at a different lunch table Monday?"

She laughed quietly and replied, "There's not room for all of us." She waved her arm slowly as if to dramatize her point.

Cars that passed drove by slowly. Some of the people we saw were people we knew, and some were not. From one direction I saw my father headed our way. He agreed he would pick us up since Mr. Carter delivered us earlier. We had agreed to meet off the roadside in the school lot.

We had just crossed school property into the parking lot when Codger Menke pulled up in the same place, obviously in a hurry. Jeremy had been waiting for him not far from us. Unlike his grandson earlier, when Mr. Menke saw me a snarl formed on his lips that I could see through the car window. He quickly climbed out of his car. I don't know why I remember it, but I remember that he was unshaven, and he wore a red baseball cap. I also recall that his fly was open, but there's a reason why that is still fresh in my mind. What a sight!

He called to his grandson loudly. He did it on purpose I think. I began to see a reason why Jeremy was like he was for so many years.

"Jeremy, get over here! I haven't got all day."

By now several cars had pulled in the lot, and several parents were part of the audience about to witness Codger's performance. For the most part, my classmates caught most of it, but I know they told their parents what they saw and heard once they got in their own vehicles or returned home. The story was throughout the school by Monday afternoon.

Walking towards his grandfather, Jeremy passed the two of us quickly. The entire time we worked that morning, he had never spoken a word to either Netty or me. Much to our surprise, as he hustled by he said to us without looking, "Thanks for coming."

That was it. We looked at each other in mild disbelief. Then the show started.

"What did you just say to the McGee boy?" Codger yelled. "What did you say?" He pointed right at me. "What is that McGee kid doing here in the first place? He doesn't live in town."

It was easy to see that Jeremy was embarrassed. His head was lowered, much like a dog puts its head down when it is scolded. I felt terrible. He actually shook. Netty and I watched him stand there and take his grandfather's abuse.

Seconds later he yelled at his grandson again. "I'm talking to you, Jeremy!" It was clearly a show of power. Jeremy was expected to toe the mark, and his grandfather did not care who witnessed it.

By now, everyone in the lot was watching a sad, ugly event take place, so I know they all heard what my dad said to Codger as he got out of our truck. He spoke firmly and clearly, as if he had a point to make.

"No you're not, Codger." My dad was angry. "You are *not* talking to your grandson. You're berating him, and for what? For saying 'Thank you' to someone who came to help you out."

It was like a tennis match. Everyone there watched my dad as he spoke, and then they looked in the opposite direction to hear what Codger Menke had to say in return.

The older man, red-faced, stared a bit before he spoke in order to collect his thoughts. Politics had trained him for such encounters. His thoughts were not nice ones.

"Well well well! If it isn't the son of Wayne County's famous runaway!" He stood there akimbo with his chin stuck out. "Your old man just left you and your mother without an apology."

I could not believe he said that to my dad. More to the point, I could not believe my dad kept his cool and came back with words that were even more cool than his composure.

"Codger Menke," he snapped as he nodded at Jeremy, "you don't deserve a grandson like this young man." My dad paused. I don't think it was for effect. I think at that moment he was trying really hard to not remove Mr. Menke's head.

"If not for him, most of these volunteers would not be here today. How can you not be grateful for that?"

Then my dad finished the entire confrontation with the words I will not *ever* forget.

"And to top off everything else," and at this point I *am sure* my father paused for effect, "your zipper is down."

Oh my God! Yes, my father knew all about Jeremy's methods in school during the past week, but he also knew

Codger would never admit in front of everyone that he had coached his own grandson to bully kids into showing up. And he was certainly not going to hang around and zip up his fly in front of everyone.

For a moment, in tennis terminology, it appeared that Dad had scored a point and won the set. Much to the surprise of everyone who witnessed his meltdown, Jeremy's grandfather motioned at him, indicating he wanted him in the car pronto, and hopped into his car as well. My father...my hero... had won the match!

CHAPTER 37

Two days later Jeremy Teller was absent from school for the first time since anyone could remember. For many, his not being there was a reprieve. A canceled dentist appointment brought less relief. The cafeteria was no less active, however. Some of the tough guys felt it incumbent to pick up Jeremy's slack, but in truth that had been going on a lot the past few weeks. Everyone at our table, the "coeds" as Jeremy himself had dubbed us, felt there was no doubt that something was going on in his head. He was just acting differently.

"Maybe he's just so embarrassed by his grandfather's behavior that he didn't want to show his face," Matt offered above the many voices in the cafeteria. "I was standing across the street in my yard, and even I could hear all that was said from there." Then basketball style, he shot an Oreo Mini into my soup.

Picking the cookie out, I popped it into my mouth. Then I yelled to Matt, "We could have heard his yelling above all of this!" I spread my arms out and looked around to make my point.

Attempting to ignore my having eaten a chocolate cookie laced with tomato soup, Jolene, one of Netty's girlfriends, chipped in, "Believe it or not, I have to feel a bit sorry for him. I think he's been trying to be nicer."

"Nicer to you maybe," Todd mentioned, "but not to everyone. Remember that preppy he tripped not too long ago?"

"That's true, but I heard he was dared to do it," added Netty. "When you think of what weight a dare carries among those creeps, he almost had to trip the guy whether he wanted to trip him or not." Jolene nodded in agreement.

Twenty-four hours later Jeremy was once again a lead topic for discussion at our table. He was absent for the second day in a row. Obviously none of us had attempted calling or texting him to ask about his welfare, but we were just as nosey as the next kid. After all, this was not just any old kid we were discussing. This guy was Bully One on the hit parade. Then Todd shared something that made me think scary thoughts.

"About two months ago," Todd began, "Mark Dodson and I decided to play golf with Teller and his grandfather." Everyone stopped chewing and talking to hear about this.

"Wait a minute," I said. "The two of you actually *chose* to play golf with both of them?"

"It's not what you think," Todd answered. "You guys don't play golf, so you are not aware of what it takes to get on the golf course in town. For Mark and me to play at the club, we have to be invited by members."

"And Mr. Menke is a member."

"Right. He gave Jeremy his permission to invite us," Todd recalled. "Then he challenged the two of us to a match."

"A match?" Netty asked.

"Yes, he insisted that he and Jeremy would play against Mark and me." Todd went on to explain how Codger Menke could be heard scolding his grandson most of the day because the boys were beating them.

Then I asked, "So how did it turn out?"

"Well, that's kinda my point." Todd's eyes enlarged, and he leaned in toward our group. "It was bad enough while they were losing. Some of his trash talking was annoying.

"But in the end, we whipped their sorry butts, and the old man went bonkers on Jeremy."

"What did he say?" we all asked excitedly.

Todd looked at us as we stared at him. "In so many words, he actually told Jeremy that he was never more ashamed of him. It bothered him so much that we had won the match that Mr. Menke insisted Jeremy buy us the sodas we had wagered."

"All of that over sodas?" one of our friends questioned.

"Yeah, like it was some big deal. He stormed off, and we never saw him again. We told Jeremy to forget the drinks. It wasn't a big deal." Then Todd added, "Here's the sad part: Jeremy didn't have enough money anyway."

"How did you find that out?" I inquired.

"He admitted it to us."

Immediate Jolene jumped in the conversation. "See that! He *has* been trying to change! The old Teller would *never* have admitted that to anyone."

Before I went to bed that Monday night, I told my parents what my friends had discussed at lunch. Their reaction told me they knew something, too.

My mom broke the news. It was awful.

"Jake," she said to me sadly, "there's been another school shooting reported on the news tonight."

Several channels, of course, carried the story. They told me what they knew.

Once again, a distraught young man with some kind of revenge in mind chose to enter his school with a hand gun in his bag. It was unclear as to whether or not his victims were premeditated, or if the assailant took the lives of young teens who happened to be in his path. As in many cases, the shooter turned his gun on himself as well.

"Where did it happen?" I asked.

They looked at each other, and they told me details. My parents told me that the shooting had taken place not too far away from Wayne County.

Dad put down his journal and muted our television. Every night he liked to record odds and ends about his day; a family historical record of sorts. "It happened in Old Church, Pennsylvania."

"Pennsylvania? Is it far from here? How badly were people hurt?" Then I caught a vibe. "Wait...you don't think–"

"We don't think anything," my mom cut me off.

I extended my hand as if asking Mom to hear me out. I had to finish my thought to make sure they knew what I was thinking.

"You don't think Jeremy would consider doing such a thing. Do you?"

With a worried countenance, Mom whispered, "We certainly hope not."

As we continued discussing Jeremy and the relationship he had with his grandfather, discussing the things we had recently witnessed and how they might affect a fourteen year old boy, we missed a brief report on the news regarding something that would have been of no interest to most people. Then again, we were not most people. Since the television had been muted, we missed a briefly detailed segment regarding the appearance and disappearance of small stone bridges around the nation.

CHAPTER 38

Much to my relief, the following day Jeremy showed up at school. I might have been the only person happy to see him who was not a member of his clique. For a while, I did not speak to Netty regarding my talk with my parents, and I am not sure why. Perhaps I did not want to scare her. I knew that I would tell her eventually, but in my mind the time had to be right. Briefly I wondered if her parents had considered whether or not Jeremy was unstable enough to consider such a horrible act.

More than ever before, I kept a close watch on him. Without his knowing, I watched what came out of his book bag, and I carefully observed what went into his locker. I even followed him and a few others into the boys lavatory before homeroom in the event someone was going to bring him something nobody should have in the building.

Of course, I could not watch him everywhere he went since we shared no class except gym, so the next time I saw him was at lunch. That's when I noticed the first change in him, the first visible changes.

To begin with, he was not wearing his grandfather's campaign button anymore. The most glaring change that day was seeing Jeremy Teller sitting with students other than the bullies. He was among the jocks! But to me, if he was in deed going to begin a personal alteration to this lifestyle, joining the jocks made a little sense since he was on the school's golf team. I wondered why he had never sat with them before.

"Good for him," I mumbled to no one in particular.

"What?" asked Netty.

I was surprised she heard me, for I really had not said it too loudly.

"Oh, I was just noticing Teller's new seat. Do you think one of the teachers made him move?"

She craned her neck as she asked, "Where is he?" Then she saw him. Big kid that he was he was easy to spot. "Oh, I see him. Interesting location."

"Not really. He does play golf," I added.

The rest of the lunch period went the same as any other day. Things were covertly tossed, people laughed loudly, notes were passed and some were intercepted. Those were like trophies or newsflashes to an eighth grader.

I pointed out to our coed group that Jeremy had moved, and how the bullies, male and female alike, never missed a beat without him. I wondered aloud how long his new choice of seating would last.

To that, Todd wondered in return, "Do you think they will ever have the guts to bust on him?"

"Are you kidding?" Jolene quipped. "It's probably already on Facebook with pix."

"They can't use their cells in here," Netty followed innocently.

"Oh yeah," Jolene remarked, "like that's going to stop them."

I saw Jeremy in gym class last period of the day, so I was able to easily keep my eye on him at day's end when the dismissal bell rang. I had to catch my bus out of town, but I had time to watch him at his locker. He did nothing out of the ordinary, but I did note that he was alone by his usual standards. No bullies, no posse, just Jeremy. Down the steps and out the front door he went. I lost sight of him quickly among all the kids in the bus line.

I woke up the following day achy. I just did not feel right. I told Gramma when she passed my room.

"I'll let your mom know," she said. "You stay there a minute. I think she's on the phone."

A few minutes later I heard my mother climb the stairs quickly, and she entered my room.

"Good morning, Jake," she said softly. "You're not feeling so great either?"

"Somebody else is sick, Mom?" I asked as I picked up my head, roused with curiosity.

She sat on the edge of my bed and placed her palm on my forehead. "I was just on the phone with Mrs. Carter." Then she plumped my pillow for me as she continued. "She said Netty was sick, and she asked if you'd get her homework for her."

"Ok," I said. I started to get out of bed.

"Where do you think you're going?" my mom asked as she put her hand on my shoulder. "You're not going to school either. You have a fever."

"Mom, you didn't even use the thermometer," I argued mildly until I realized how woozy I felt when I sat up too quickly.

"I'll get the thermometer, Bucko," she laughed, "but I know just by feeling your forehead that you have a temperature."

As the morning passed, I dozed. I don't know why, but at one point I wondered if this was why Teller stayed home. No one had the guts to ask him where he had been. Then I became worried. I actually wondered if his mean grandfather had done something abusive to him.

On a whim, I emailed Netty from my laptop. Since I was stuck in bed, Mom let me have it to pass the time. That was very "un-Mom" -like. Both she and Mrs. Carter where adamant about limiting our use of our computers. In fact, Netty and I were among the few in our middle school who did not have our own cell phone. I shot off a note.

Netty, I hear ur not feeling so great. Hope ur better soon.

I want to share something with u since we can write in private.

It was then that I shared the details of my conversation that I had with my parents two nights ago. When I had finished, I presented her with the question I wanted to ask her twenty-four hours earlier:

Do you think Jeremy would do something like that?

And then my final question:

Do you think he stayed home two days because his grandfather smacked him and left marks?

I sent the note to her about 10:20 that morning. Three minutes later I received her reply.

> *Believe it or not, Jake, we had the same talk! I didn't now how to discuss it with you yesterday. I don't know why. Scared I guess.*
> *I wanted to believe it would never happen to kids in our school.*
> *But it could, couldn't it?*

Then she answered my second question.

> *I didn't see any marks on him, but I wasn't looking for any.*
> *His grandfather is so mean. I bet he might be able to do such a horrible thing. I hope not.*

The rest of our emails were in part about Jeremy, but for the most part they were about getting back out into the woods. We agreed that the disappearance of the stone bridge had to mean something, and we were anxious to find it again. By 11:00 we stopped emailing, because both of us were pretty zonked.

CHAPTER 39

It was Thursday night. I will never forget it. As if my malady had passed almost as quickly as it had arrived, I felt much better. Stronger actually.

"I want to go back to school tomorrow," I said to my mom when I entered the kitchen. Then briefly I thought again about Jeremy. He had been out two days. Perhaps he *was* hiding scars or bruises.

"Want a snack? Some soup?" Mom asked.

Dad walked in. "How ya feelin'?" he asked as he patted me on the back gently. Without waiting for my answer he went on to say, "We were able to speak to a forester today. Thought you'd be interested."

"Does he know what a forester is?" Mom asked Dad.

I looked at my father. "Actually she's right. I have no idea what you mean." I sat down at the table and watched my mother cutting something.

"Oh! A forester is a man or woman who oversees the Game Lands."

My interest piqued. My father was talking about the bridge in the woods.

"What did you find out?"

"Not a lot." My dad sat down opened his thermos. "He was surprised that anyone saw a bridge like you described in the forest. Never heard of such a thing." He finished what little juice he had left.

I wondered if the forester took my claim seriously, and I suspect my father knew I was wondering that very thing. My dad knew me like a book.

"I have to give him credit," he added. "He even took the time to show me a topographical map."

"Why?"

Dad continued as Mom brought each of us the last two pieces of that chocolate cake. "Using both the topo map on paper and the topo map on his computer, we were able to study any possible drainage areas. We both agreed that the maps indicate that there's never been enough drainage to require a bridge of any type."

"That's really weird." Then I had a thought. "How old were the maps? When were they made?"

He understood my thought process. "That's a good question. I really don't know, but I see what you're getting at. Land forms might have changed over time.

"I'll see him again for ya," and then we both attacked our snack.

I said, "Good night" to my folks, but not before asking, "Where's Gramma?"

"This afternoon she said she had some errands to run," my mother told me. "But now that you mention it, she is a little late coming back."

Dad did not sound too worried about his mom, but he asked, "Didn't she say where she was headed?"

"She was pretty vague, to be honest. Almost secretive." My mother collected the dirty plates. "I wondered if she was arranging some sort of surprise for one of us, but our birthdays are not for quite some time, and Christmas is two months away."

We opted to wait and see. Dad said he would take a drive up and down the road in case she broke down if she wasn't back home soon.

I went up to bed. It's funny how a person can do almost nothing physically demanding all day, but he can still be tired enough to fall asleep. It was well after midnight when the sound of a short siren and some voices woke me up.

All it took was the sight of red and blue lights flashing on my bedroom wall to make my knees buckle. I felt weak. I felt nauseous. I *knew* something bad had happened, but I was afraid to leave the safety net my room provided. I wanted to know what was going on, and at the same time I did *not* want to know what was going on. Finally I just sucked it up and walked slowly down the stairs into our living room.

My mom saw me first, and got up to meet me arms wide open. In a heartbreaking tone she gasped, "Oh, Jake!"

"Mom, what's going on? Why are all these people here?" I looked across the room at my father. He held his head in his hands. I could not see the expression on his face but knew it was not pleasant.

Maybe it was selfish, but I called to him, "Dad! What's going on?"

He looked up, and I saw tears in my father's eyes for the first time since Grampa's disappearance. He opened his mouth, but no words came out. Mom led me to his side.

"It's happened again," he finally sobbed. "Jake, it's happened again."

I looked up at my mother. "What's he talking about, Mom?"

Three other men, police officers, were in the room. None of them said a word. Then Mr. Carter came through our front door.

"Dan, I got here as fast as I could. What can I do to help?"

My dad stood up and hugged Mr. Carter. Grown men were exchanging softy spoken condolences and exchanging hugs.

To Netty's dad my father said, "Thanks, Jack. There's nothing we can do until daylight. The officers are already organizing search parties so they will be ready to go."

"Search parties?" I whispered to myself. "Who's missing here?"

I looked around the living room and found the flashing of lights upon our walls unnerving, but there was more. Gramma was not anywhere to be seen. That is when I understood. Gramma had disappeared just like my grandfather. I now understood my father's disconsolate words. "Jake, it's happened again."

CHAPTER 40

As best I could, I stayed out of the way. Sleep, of course, was out of the question. As dawn approached, more and more volunteers and rescue personnel showed up. Once again our driveway was filled with emergency vehicles. Yes, déjà vu had come to the McGee home.

Despite not being directly involved, I was able to eavesdrop enough to learn that Gramma's car was found down a dirt road that led into the Game Lands not far from our property. From what I could discern from snippets of official conversations among the officers, there was no sign of a struggle or foul play, but the keys were missing. Perhaps Gramma took something from the trunk which required using her trunk key on her old car, and out of habit she might have taken the keys with her to where she was headed.

Of course, that kind of thinking accompanied the theory that she chose to depart, and that she had not been kidnapped. I could not decide which was worse until I realized along with kidnapping came the possibility of resistance followed by physical harm. But why in the world would Gramma *choose* to leave us; just walking away and not saying a word made no sense to me.

Sitting by a large window, I was processing a lot in my head. I wondered if Mr. Carter had told his wife yet. Did Netty know? Sure she did. He must have told them. I began to figure the only reason my mother's best friend was not present was because they had no place to leave Netty who probably was still ill. They certainly would not leave her alone under these awful circumstances. Netty loved Gramma as if she was her own. We all knew that.

No sooner had that concept run through my head when Mrs. Carter showed up with Netty. "As if on cue!" I thought to myself. I got up from my seat to meet them.

I was at the door when I saw Netty come up the front steps on to the veranda behind her mom. My mother was hugging Mrs. Carter as if she would not let go. I saw Netty peek by them, looking for me. When our eyes met, she passed them by quickly and ran into my arms. Even under these circumstances I thought, "This is a first!" We led them into the house.

Without saying a word, we mutually chose to stay downstairs with all of the adults. To scoot up to my room meant risking the missing of any announcements. Instead, we sat on our couch side by side. My best friend took my hand gently and did not let go. Her fearful eyes wide open, she did not mind if anyone saw us.

Netty and I were silent. We just kept watching and listening. The sky was beginning to brighten, and we could hear the rescue teams organizing, adopting equal numbers of non-professionals to support their search parties. And, just like the first time six years earlier, they began dividing up the search area into grids.

Over the din of Search Party radios, I heard Mrs. Carter utter to my mother, "May I borrow your phone? I want to call the courthouse and tell them I won't be coming in."

To that my mom replied, "And we have to remember to call the school, or they'll be calling us about the kids being absent."

The wheels in my head went around. Gently I whispered, for I cared not to startle Netty, "Oh geez. Once our Moms call in, they're going to have to give reasons. *Then* the news will spread like wildfire."

"So?" was all that Netty said.

"So? Don't you think you-know-who will have a field day with this information?"

"Who? Who in the world would have fun with your— ooooh. I get it." The proverbial light had gone on. "Codger Menke. That's who. Right?"

"Uh huh. The man's a certified...what's that word Matt Labib always uses?"

She looked at me almost humorously and said, "Cretin."

"Yeah. Cretin." If only for a second, it was nice to see her smile.

As promised, people started out as soon as daylight permitted. Some took their vehicles to their assigned search areas while the rest just started out on foot. Unfortunately, the weather was showing its ugly side. Rain began falling, and not long after that a blustery wind kicked up. All I could hope was that Gramma was sheltered not only from harm's way, but also the lousy weather.

The house had quieted for the most part. Mr. Carter and my dad insisted on joining one of the search parties. I wanted to go as well, but that was ruled out. I was definitely upset when I was told I would be of more value if I stayed behind.

"Dad, how can I help from the house?" I argued. It was unusual for me to squabble, and he knew it. He realized I was as upset as he was.

"Jake, I'm going to speak to you man-to-man. I don't know who or what we're going to find out there. I can't control it. But I do know this: if it's ugly, I do *not* want you to witness it."

His words set me back. Reality slapped me hard. I watched him leave, and I never did get an answer from him. What could I say? He was looking out for me. I knew that. Gramma was probably out there in the woods. She might be found, and the discovery might not be pretty. I had not considered the possibility of another unhappy ending.

CHAPTER 41

To occupy her mind, Mom had managed to make all four of us some hot chocolate. It is odd how little things can be comforting during such a tragedy. A cup of hot chocolate, a friendly word, or just holding hands. Little things can mean a lot.

My radar up, I honed in on my mother's words to Mrs. Carter. "Lil, I think you should get Netty back home. She's not herself, but then again who is?" She took her friend's two hands in hers and said, "I love you for being here, and you're welcome to stay, but we really need to take care of her, too." Mom was right. As much as I did not want to see her leave, I had to admit that she looked washed out.

I could tell Mrs. Carter was torn. She didn't want Netty to become more ill, but she wanted to be here to support my mom.

"Lil, go. Really."

"Ok, but you have to promise to call me as soon as—"

"Of course," and then she added, "and when she's up to it, get back over here. The two of you are good for the two of us." With that they hugged, put Netty's coat upon her, and they departed. I watched as they hiked up our long driveway, Mrs. Carter's arm around her daughter, and I began feeling inept as a friend. I wanted to help make her better but I did not know how.

"Mom, can I ask you something?"

"Of course, Sweetheart," she said as we both waved to them when they turned and looked back.

"When did Netty get so pretty?"

"Oh, Jake. Don't you start growing up on me so fast." We turned and walked back to the house arm in arm. Mom leaned into me and said, "It hasn't happened over night."

"Gramma told me the same thing."

It drizzled off and on throughout the morning hours. The sky was light gray and the rain darkened each tree's branches, stripped of leaves by autumn winds. Early afternoon brought a cold, heavier rain that fell more steadily, and I was going stir crazy. The temporary excitement of an occasional radio broadcast broke the monotony.

The phone rang quite a few times. Each time was equally scary. We did not want bad news, but we had to take the calls regardless. While Mom spent more time than usual fielding questions from one particular friend, an idea crept into my head. I made up my mind that no matter how much trouble I might get into, I was going out into those woods.

"Who knows them better than I do?" I thought to myself. My bold decision fizzled as soon as Mom finished her phone chat. I could not bring myself to do it. Mom would be even more upset, and that was something that would make me feel bad.

I thought of other things, but finally my thinking came around to just why my grandmother would up and leave. I actually whispered to myself, as I watched the rain against my bedroom window, droplets snaking their way to the sill, "Why would she park her car where she did? Who was she meeting? Was she looking for something? Was she looking for —

"Oh my God! The Game Lands!" It hit me like a lightning bolt. "She's going after Grampa! She's been in touch with him!" Temporarily I grew weak. Then I had to decide what to do regarding my own mother. Do I tell her? Do I email Netty? The answer to both was an emphatic "No!"

Immediately I started gathering the gear we always took. I had second thoughts. I could make a call to Netty about this, but it was nearly 1:30, and daylight was wasting. It would take too long for her to get here. And if I *did* have her mom bring her to our house, making our moms understand would be impossible. Our mothers would never let us go, especially with Netty being sick. I had to go it alone. My mom would be upset, but now I was driven. I could live with any punishment, because I knew I could find Gramma and bring her home.

As if delivered by fate, the distraction I needed came in the person of James Hamill, reporter for our local television station's news team, WNEP. James was the Honesdale High graduate who often covered stories across Wayne County, including the mysterious disappearance of my grandfather six years earlier when his career first began. I had never met him, but recognizing him was easy. A local folk legend of sorts, he once attended our schools, and my parents and I saw him every week in our living room.

Mom remembered James's kindness from years ago, and immediately granted him another interview which ended up taking place over our kitchen table. I am sure he was thinking a double disappearance six years apart might be of great interest to his audience, especially since the people who vanished were husband and wife, but he also felt that by informing his station's viewing audience, together they were increasing the chances of Gramma being spotted.

I could not let the opportunity slip by. As quietly as I could, I went down our steps, across our living room, and out the door. Toward the shed out back, I walked as casually as I could so as to attract no attention. I even waved at one of the volunteers whose job it was to man the radios on the porch. I walked inside the big, gray, wooden shed through its front door, closed it behind me, and I raced out the back. It was 1:45, so I figured I had three hours of daylight at most.

Out of nowhere, I heard the crashing of footsteps through the tall grass behind me. I could not believe my eyes. As if he was reading my mind, Artie had somehow escaped the house as well and tore right by me. I did not doubt that he knew what I was doing and where I was going. Without a sound, he made it clear I was not going without him.

"Find Gramma!" I yelled as he continued to increase his lead, but somehow I knew I really did not have to tell him. There was no zigzagging through the woods on this day. His path was straight and true like that of a laser beam. Rocks and bushes phased him not.

More to help me than anything else, Artie began his howling in thirty-second intervals. It was the only way I could tell where he wanted me to follow. Unlike the last time he commanded such a pace, the hills did not bother me. I needed no rest breaks. Up and down woodsy hillocks we raced.

I found it odd that not one member of any search party was to be encountered as we ran. On the fly, I reasoned perhaps this particular quadrant and others like it might have been already explored earlier in the day. At the moment of my first stumble down the side of one hill, I was beginning to wish I had some help. It was not a gentle, slow-rolling kind of wipe out. I saw rocks and tree trunks whoosh by my head, but miraculously I popped back up and was on my way once again.

This second chase went on for more than an hour. I looked at my watch, and it was now 3:10 p.m. Under the gray sky and in this forest, I knew it would be darkening soon. Ahead of me I spotted some boulders that looked vaguely familiar. Then a cluster of pines came into view, and I was certain Artie and I had been here before. Despite the thunder of my own big feet, once again I noted the howling had stopped.

As I came out of the pines, there he was. He was once again waiting for me as he did the day we first discovered the bridge. The bridge! Artie had once again led me to the old, single-arch fieldstone bridge! However this time he acted differently. Artie ambled toward it as if curious or careful. I followed with equal care. After all the running we had done, a slow walk felt good. The air was still, and the rain had stopped falling. Until that moment, I had not even noticed. There was just something surreal about this part of the entire forest.

CHAPTER 42

As expected, darkness began having its effect early due to cloud coverage. I also knew that returning to our property was going to require my navigating the woods well after dark. As far as rule-breaking goes? I was about to make Teller and the boys look like boy scouts. No detention they ever served would compare to the one I was facing.

Standing there, looking all about me, I did not even care about any punishment I was facing or the worry I might cause. I knew there was a reason I was there. I knew there was a reason Artie chose where to bring me. I just had to ride it out. It all became worth it when I heard Grampa's voice. No signals. No flags. I heard his voice.

"You're a smart little whipper," he said. The message was definitely not telepathic. I actually was hearing my grandfather's voice. "You're a bit stubborn, too. A real McGee, through and through."

And *that* was when I heard Gramma's reserved laughter followed by, "I told you he was growing up to be like you, Jacob."

A flash of light exploded across the entire area. It formed a dome nearly fifty yards in diameter and stood approximately one hundred feet tall at its peak. Darkness outside the dome surrounded it. The light was not of the blinding sort some movies portray in stories about aliens. It was more of a mini sunrise; everything green or brown taking on a golden hue.

In the middle of the dome of light stood my grandparents. Again, their appearance was not the spectacle I had seen in motion pictures where angel-like figures possess an aura about them. I saw my grandparents standing in the woods as if it was early morning.

"Aren't you happy to finally see me?" he asked.

"Grampa, I have so many questions," was my first response. Not exactly how I had planned the joyous dialogue I sometimes rehearsed in my head for years when I could not sleep. My grandparents understood.

"Jacob, I can't imagine what is going through your mind, but let me try to put you at ease." He motioned for me to step upon the bridge. I failed to notice that Artie was already at his master's side.

"Can't you come down here?" I asked. I was shaking more than a little, because I was more than a little leery of them. Were these two figures really my grandparents?

"OK then, let's start with that," he replied. His voice had not changed one bit since last I saw him. I wondered how that was possible along with the fact that he looked the same, too.

"Start with what?"

"Let me tell you about my new world." Gramma stood beside him with her arm tucked inside his own.

"World?" I exclaimed. "You're in a different world?" This was beginning to really weird me out. My grandfather sensed it.

"Jake, a long time ago, before you were born, I was offered the opportunity to do what I loved to do best: take care of living things."

I started to say something, but he held up his hand.

"Let me talk a bit," he said. "For now we have fifty pounds of talking to do, and we only have ten pounds of time in which to do it.

"Over millions of years, for various reasons, some species of animals became extinct...in the world of men. By the grace of God, I get to help care for them in a place, a world, where they live free of predators and disease."

I approached the bridge as he spoke, and I finally found the courage to end up hugging both of them. We sat upon the stones of the bridge as if it were a bench. My feet dangled a little. His reached the ground. He was still a large figure. My grandmother leaned comfortably against the arched wall as he continued.

"Growing up," he said, "you learned how much I loved the forest. I tried to pass that along to you."

"Did Gramma know this offer you were given? The opportunity presented to you?" I was machine gunning my questions. "Why not your own son? Why not pass it on to him?" Gramps was patient. He knew he had to account for some things.

"Yes, she knew it. And as for your daddy?" He paused. "He already had you and your mom. I could not take him from the two of you."

"Go on."

"This bridge that Artie has shown you is a gate created for extinct and endangered animals to join us. Its appearance is more cosmetic than anything. The design is believed to be more inviting than one of those Sci-fi portals we have all seen on the television."

"What do you mean, Gramps?"

He paused and thought. "Animals recognize bridges for what they are; a natural path to get to where they want to be. Not all bridges are man-made." He pointed across the woods. "Downed trees can be bridges."

That made sense.

"And why do you think Artie's friend the Minorcan Giant, the big rabbit, was here?" Gramps chuckled when he asked.

"To cross over." That part I understood. "But what about Gramma?"

I looked at her. "Gramma, why didn't you tell us?"

Putting her hands upon my shoulders, she spoke to me about her decision to be with her husband.

"I could have departed with Grampa long ago, Jacob." Tears formed in her eyes. I could see them.

"But I wanted to be sure the three of you were going to be okay." She tried to make a joke and said with a chuckle, "I knew this old geezer would be all right. I had been given assurances. It was you who I worried about. Now I am no longer worried."

I stood up. Even in this perfect world of theirs, my butt still became sore from sitting on stone.

"Ok. I accept that. But I have to ask." I struggled with the wording of my next question, for its meaning was of great importance to me. I wanted to get it right. I needed to word it perfectly.

"If you knew you were going to see Grampa again, does that mean we'll get to see the two of you again as well?"

They both smiled the happiest smiles I had ever seen. Gramma nodded at Grampa, a signal that evidently meant that she wanted him to answer me.

"Yes, Jacob. As long as it's what you want." It was a cryptic answer, but I could live with cryptic.

"I'll get to see you again...Mom and Dad will get to see you both again?"

They both answered this time, "Yes, if it's what you want."

I sensed they had little time left, and there was so much more I wanted to discuss. They were patient enough to answer more questions, but I could not think of everything.

I really feared sounding disrespectful, but I had to probe more deeply.

"Gramps, people spent weeks looking for you. Now they will do it all over again looking for Gramma." I looked at my grandmother. The passive look on her face could have been interpreted in many ways. But I had to ask. "How can you let them search knowing they might be injured?"

"That's a pretty adult thought, my boy," he said to me. "I'm proud of you. You're thinking of others." He took a deep breath and asked me to trust him. He asked me to have faith. And then he said, "I've been promised no harm will come to anyone."

Only because he was my grandfather, I thought I could accept that. However, I needed clarity.

"So when I get back," I continued, "searches will continue for a spell."

"And no one will be injured. I promise." He actually looked skyward and said, "It has to be this way, Jake."

"May I ask one more thing before you go?"

"Of course," said my namesake. "Ask it."

"How am I ever going to explain this to Mom and Dad?"

His answer brought me tremendous relief. The kind of relief one feels when he or she wakes from that awful dream about the pop quiz, learning it was all just that: a dream.

He extended his hand. "First of all, wait for a private moment and give them these." He handed me their wedding rings on the gold chain Gramma had always worn around her neck. My mother had given it to her as an anniversary gift years ago.

"This last part is most important: After you give them our rings, direct them to the family Bible. We'll take care of the rest."

My grandparents hugged me a final time, and Grampa walked me to the bottom of the bridge.

"I can go no farther," he said to me. "It's one of the truths to which I agreed." His final words to me that day were, "We love you, Jake. Please be happy for all of us." Later I wondered if he meant the animals or our family.

As the grandfather I love turned to walk back up the old stone bridge, I looked over his shoulder and saw my grandmother blow me a kiss. Then they were gone. No sign of the bridge could be spotted. No signs of any animals wanting to cross over the bridge were evident, yet I knew that was why my grandparents had been there. Or was Gramma the only one crossing that day?

My eyes adjusted quickly. It was not as dark as I thought it would be. I looked at my watch and only a few minutes had passed. Had Grampa been able to somehow slow down time? I approached what was once the stone bridge. It had been reduced to a pile of rocks. There was nothing preternatural about them that would draw any outdoorsman's attention. Despite the late hour, despite knowing full darkness was approaching, I sat down to absorb what I had just witnessed.

CHAPTER 43

All I had left were expensive, gold trinkets. I fingered their wedding rings set upon Gramma's gold chain for a bit, and then secured them in a zippered pocket inside the yellow, light-weight jacket I was wearing over my burgundy hooded sweater. At that moment, the emotions running through me were diverse. Of course, after years of searching I was happy to know that Gramps was alive. Too, I was saddened that I would not see him for a time.

"Alive". Now there is a term I had to ponder. His new existence proffered a whole new meaning. I settled for accepting a normal definition of "alive". After all, I was able to hug both of them. They felt real and "alive".

Then there was Gramma to consider. She was alive and reunited with Grampa. I knew I should feel happy for her. I began to appreciate the patience she exhibited having waited for six whole years to be with her husband again! Also I felt her love for us was even more evident once I knew she gave up those six years just to make sure we were going to be okay. As I sat there in the woods upon a pile of rocks where the bridge had stood moments ago, I became increasingly more grateful for her sacrifice. I knew she had done the right thing by staying behind. Losing both parents would have been even more horrific for her own son back then.

When I stood I simply said, "Let's go home, Artie." As we walked by that now-familiar stand of pines, I wondered how to deal with the sadness that I felt as well, sad that it would most likely be quite some time before all of us were together again.

The entire post-dome experience became an emotional roller coaster, for I had to admit it was wonderful to know our reunion was a certainty. Gramps had said, "As long as it's what you want." Of course, I wanted to be with them again. Why would I not?

It was impossible to establish the pace we had set racing into the woods earlier that afternoon. Despite having my hand-held floodlight, it was tricky walking in the forest at dusk. Knowing it would soon be flat-out dark, I had to be extra careful about my footing.

Artie must have sensed my predicament, for he stayed near me the entire time. The darkness and the terrain were seemingly not a threat to him.

Shortly after we began our return, I began to worry about my reception. Why hadn't I thought of it sooner? No one was going to find Gramma. That was for sure. Any efforts by the rescue teams would be futile. They did not know that, and I knew I would began feeling terrible if any of them were injured during the search. It sickened me to even consider facing the Search and Rescue squads. I knew what Grampa said, but how could he prevent such an occurrence?

There was more. If I did not return by dark, they were going to begin searching for me as well. I worried that when they found me, if they found me, I would be in trouble deep.

"Even if Mom and Dad believe me," I said to Artie, "what will we tell everyone else?"

I was sure the gift of my grandparents' jewelry would fill them with wonder. It was the presence of a letter in the family Bible that was to placate them. What had he written?

Things suddenly became worse. With my mind wandering and wondering like it was, my focus upon my hiking was minimized. I can only guess, but I suppose I slipped carelessly upon some moss the afternoon rain had made treacherous.

Before I knew it, my feet were nearly above my head and instinctively I dropped my lamp, extended my arms to cushion my fall, and prepared myself for what might happen in that next instant. In the darkness, I began a rapid, sliding descent down a rough embankment I had not realized was adjacent to the path where seconds prior I had absentmindedly been stepping. I rolled once and did more sliding as I began picking up momentum. My arms and legs were flailing when suddenly I stopped.

I was not even close to being prepared for the horrific pain that ensued. In a heartbeat, I halted awkwardly and felt the back of my calf being punctured. It was but a stroke of good fortune that my flood lamp tumbled into ground cover within my reach, and it did not power down upon its own impact.

For but a brief second, I tried to lie still and assess what I had done by falling. The pain was excruciating. How badly was I hurt? I knew right away that my injury was of a serious nature. I had hoped the immediate pain would pass or at least abate, but it didn't. It was relentless. I had to fight from squirming, for movement made the agony worse.

All of this happened in the first five or ten seconds after I slipped. At the tick of the next second of time, I began screaming like I had never cried out before. Despite the exhaustion immediately set upon me by the screaming and the pain, an inner force enabled me to attempt a reach for my lamp. I thought I had seen my last sunrise; actually experienced a life-flashes-before-my-eyes moment. Excruciating pain coursed through the lower part of my left leg causing me to nearly lose my breath.

I had to try again. Securing the lamp, I knew, was a must. The pace of my second attempt to grasp the lamp rivaled the movement of the minute hand upon my grandfather's pocket watch which he let me hold long ago. Barely detectable but in constant motion, my fingers finally touched the yellow handle near the beam of light I sought.

It rolled further into the ground cover, but only an inch or two. How long I was in that position, summoning up the courage to reach out for my light, I know not. My desire to secure the lamp at any cost intensified. Right then and there, I needed to be successful or my will to continue might have been threatened. I counted, "One...two..."

As if a fifty pound bag of potatoes was rolling down the same embankment, my hound made his clumsy, less-than-gracious arrival at my side. By the grace of God, he knocked my lamp not further away, but nearly into my chest! For a moment, Artie moved not one iota. Perhaps he, too, was checking himself for wear and tear. Having assessed his fate, he hopped up and licked my face. Briefly it was all right and then he pushed my leg. The gut-wrenching shriek I emitted caused him to immediately back away.

"I'm sorry, Artie. I'm sorry." I sucked wind. He had not seen me like this ever before.

Despite my pain which flamed inside of my calf with the intensity of a blow torch my dad had taught me to use, by using the lamp I was able to see where a pointed branch entered the flesh on the back of my leg on one side and exited on the other. My calf was shiny from the mixture of rainfall and my own blood which continued to ooze from my wound. Of course, I needed help. I did not dare try to move. I considered snapping the branch to increase my mobility, but I opted for a more cowardly approach.

Somehow I managed to keep my wits about me, for I called Artie to my side. I had to send some sort of message that would tell everyone something was wrong. Nothing I was carrying or wearing was out of the ordinary, so I just affixed my watch to his collar. I hoped that would attract somebody's attention.

It was not an easy task, for the tiniest of movements served only to increase my pain. Once it was attached, and after several deep breaths, I said to him as clearly as I could, "Artie, you have to go home *now!*"

He took a few steps back, nearly out of the range of my lamp and looked at me. I like to think he was deciding whether or not leaving me was a good idea. To be honest, he might have been wondering about the misfit I had become.

Then he howled once and took off. For a few seconds all I heard were his footsteps, and then he began using his howl as an asset. Later I was told that his howling signal indeed had worked.

After a time, even Artie's voice evaporated into the night. I know I cried, and I'm sure I cried aloud until finally I passed out. I surely did not fall asleep. I awoke to more pain. The fire in my leg had been reignited.

"Jake! Can you hear me?" The voice sounded distant. "Jake! Wake up!"

I once had oral surgery, and I remember what it was like being awakened, for anesthesia had been used to knock me out. Hearing words in the distance again was similar, but this time a pain in my leg reduced the amount of time it took me to come to my senses.

"Jake? Jake!" Someone was putting something under my head. Finally I opened my eyes. No matter what amount of pain I was in, who I saw kneeling over me could not have summoned a greater surprise.

"Teller?" and then I screamed again. It must have startled him badly, for he fell back on his rear. It was Artie all over again. But to his credit, he was back at my side in an instant.

"Jeremy," I asked breathlessly for the pain was intense, "how did you find me? What time is it?" Again I looked around. "Are you alone?"

"Easy, Jake." Jeremy had the look of a young paramedic, as if he was deciding what needed to be done. "I think it might be best if you don't talk, but I do want you to try to stay awake."

He answered my initial questions as he surveyed my situation some more. "I heard your hound's howling, found it, and at his urging I followed him here from the middle of the woods. It took me a while to get here. I'm guessing it's about seven."

Soon it became obvious he was alone. As he talked to me, he removed one of his sweatshirts and covered me as best he could. He kneeled and leaned back as he ran his fingers through his hair, seeming unsure as to what he should do next.

"Jake, I think you're leg's hurt pretty bad." He shined my lamp upon it. "As I see it we have only a few choices."

"Teller, you are *not* going to try amputating my leg!" I said firmly as I cringed. He looked at me like I was crazy for only a second and then realized I was either joking or in some serious shock. I once read someplace that Americans do that. They paint even the ugliest scenarios with humor to temporarily buy time to think.

His comeback was equally clever. "Well, that *was* one choice."

I groaned and despite his instructions that I should limit my talking, I managed to ask him, "Tell me what you're thinking, Jer."

"Well I'll clean this the best I can, and we ride out the night here in the woods."

"And?"

"The branch through your calf isn't too old, and despite the obvious force of your fall it seems to have remained in one piece."

Holding my breath I asked, "What do you mean?"

"It means that there's only a little bit of the branch protruding from one side, and the rest of the branch is still rooted in the ground on the other side of your leg."

"Teller," I joked again, "did you just use 'protruding' in a sentence?"

He smiled briefly and said, "Jake, if you don't stop clowning around, I'm gonna just leave you here."

Then he became serious again. I can cut the branch to free up your leg. I know it would relieve the tension." I could tell he was thinking some serious thoughts, so I kept my mouth shut. After all, he seemed to know what he was doing.

"I thought about removing the stick, but that's too risky."

The fact that these words were coming out of *Jeremy Teller's* mouth was impressive. How did he know this stuff? I wondered whether or not he had some level of First Aid Training.

"The blood seems to have clotted, so I am guessing the stick has not torn open a vessel. And if it has, even a little bit, it seems to be serving as a patch, believe it or not. So moving it would be a bad idea."

He looked around, but I doubt he could see very far even with my powerful lamp. "Maybe I could rig something up and drag you out of here."

"I guess that's option three." I winced again. My leg burned so badly I worried about passing out again.

"Actually," Jeremy said, "that is the third option, but I am not leaving you alone. Somebody will find us, and if I hear them I'll be able to call them."

He asked me to lie back. "I have to cut that branch. That will help you a lot. Do you have a knife in your backpack?"

I told him I carried a Leatherman, and that there was a blade he could use or a small pliers. He cut it as quickly as he could with the blade since the branch was too flexible for a quick snap of the pliers.

The immediate decrease in pressure relaxed me, and for a while neither of us spoke. Our choices sucked. Then he came up with the idea that worked.

"Jake, do you think your dog can go find somebody else?"

For a few moments we discussed what we could attach to Artie before we sent him off. We decided Jeremy's school I.D. was the best idea. He pinned it to Artie's collar next to my watch.

"There!" he said when he was done. "Now someone will find out you are not alone."

For the second time that night, I told Artie he had to go home. Loyal hound that he was, off into the darkness he went.

CHAPTER 44

Artie's departure left just the two of us to face what might be the longest night of our lives. To get my mind off some of my pain, I wanted to talk; ask Jeremy some questions, but I didn't want to sound condescending. I picked my words carefully.

"Jeremy, in my backpack is a First Aid Kit. There should be some Tylenol in there and some water."

He helped me get those down with a drink, and I noticed him shivering.

"Jer, you're cold."

"Yeah, but you've go to wear that sweatshirt." He tucked it around me again. "Wait," he added, "you're not going to get weird on me and ask me to snuggle. Are you?"

Even though I had injured my leg, it hurt to laugh as well, but I had to laugh all the same. When I yelped and winced, he realized I felt pain. Immediately he apologized for making me laugh. "Sorry, Jake," was all he said, but it was enough, because I knew he was sincere.

"I have an idea," I carefully let escape from my lips. "I think we can get a fire going."

"Really? How are we going to do that when everything's soaked?"

I lied when I said it, but I told him that if he rounded the nearby stand of pine trees, he might find some dry stuff near the pile of rocks not far beyond.

"Why would that stuff be dry?" he asked. I'm sure he was wondering whether or not I was beginning to hallucinate.

It was right then that I lied. "Earlier today it seemed that the storm didn't soak everything here. I noticed it when I walked by that way." What I couldn't say was that my grandparents stopped by, lit up the woods with a magical dome, and dried things out a bit. Nope. I couldn't say that.

"You'll be okay while I go look?" he asked. As he stood he shared a thought. "Wait a minute. How are we going to ignite whatever I find?"

I took another slow, deep breath, winced yet again and said, "Backpack." He understood my intent, but I still couldn't understand why a leg injury was causing me pain in other parts of my body.

It could not have been more than three trips back and forth, and Jeremy had quite a pile of kindling. "Now what? he asked.

"Do you remember Mrs. Keen in second grade?"

"You're kidding. Right?"

Another deep breath. "No. I'm serious. She taught us something cool." I went on to explain that he could find a brand new nine-volt battery along with some steel wool in my pack. As she taught our class to do, I would teach Jeremy how to prepare a fire using the two together.

"Can I ask you a question, Jake?"

I nodded slowly.

"Why don't you just carry a lighter?"

I was stumped. I have to admit I felt pretty stupid. I had no answer, so I squeezed out the words, "Next time."

He stifled a laugh for fear I would laugh as well. After looking skyward for safe clearance and then clearing a place for a campfire on the ground, he followed my instructions perfectly. I instructed him to carefully let the dry grasses fine as hair touch the steel-wool wires which glowed the instant they contacted both battery posts. It took a few attempts, but once he realized he had to act quickly, we had the makings of a fire. It did not take long for him to catch on, first piling on little twigs until he had a nice bed of coals begging for bigger sticks. The entire process was uplifting.

"You know, I see you have two flares in the bag. We could have used those." Then he asked, "Your dad let you have them?"

"My dad taught me how to respect them first." I next complimented him on his suggestion, but I told him that we might need flares later to draw attention to ourselves. "They've even been used as a form of protection."

"Good point," he said. "You're pretty savvy about this outdoorsy stuff." Then he opened a door to an entirely different conversation when he said, "I admire that."

The extra Tylenol I swallowed had to be helping decrease my pain, but our conversation was helping to distract me as well. I looked at him and saw a kindness in his face as he stared at the flames of our crackling fire. Sensing a bond of sorts, sensing his guard was down, I asked him about his involvement.

"Jeremy, what were you doing out here looking for me? And why were you alone?"

The firelight revealed a pensive look on his face. I imagined it was difficult for him to answer my questions. Finally he did.

"I've been a jerk for so long, I decided a while back that I wanted to be like somebody else. I wanted to be like you. I wanted to do something good."

"What?" Even though it hurt to speak, I let my surprise boom out.

He put his fingers to his lips. "Just listen. Okay? This isn't easy for me." I nodded, and he continued.

"Even back in seventh grade I noticed some things you did to help out others. You're the kind of kid who helps others pick up books that I used to knock out of their hands." He looked ashamed when he admitted it. "You lent money to kids after I took it from them," he sighed. He paused and carefully added some more wood to the fire.

"So this past summer I set some goals for myself, and one of them was to be nicer to people." He looked at the tree tops. "It wasn't easy. The guys I hang with began busting on me, so I almost fell back into my old ways."

"Like the day you tripped the kid."

"Yeah," he admitted. "But that was the last time." More wood was added to the fire. I could tell he was nervous.

"Then when I saw you hanging with Matt Labib, helping him out, I thought that was really cool."

"Thanks." I adjusted my position a little bit so I could let another part of my body benefit from the heat of the fire. It felt nearly as good as Jeremy's compliments.

"Then last week there was that whole highway thing."

I tried to reduce the pressure he was feeling. "Yeah, we did a good thing there."

"Jake, you know what I mean. No one deserved to see my grandfather like that or hear the things he said, especially your dad." He put his head down. He was deflated.

"Hey, Jer, that wasn't your fault." I let the words settle a minute, and then I said, "No matter what he said, we did a good thing."

"Thanks."

We were quiet for a while. We could hear a breeze kicking up through the needles of the evergreens nearby. Pines do not rattle like trees with leaves, so instead there was a whispering sound...a light whirring sound.

I took another chance. I was eager to know more about the person who might have pushed me up against a locker on any other day.

"Jeremy, I was wondering. Why were you absent for two days? Were you sick like I was?"

He was wise to me immediately. "No," he said flatly. "You're wondering whether or not my grandfather smacked me Saturday. That's what you are wondering."

I didn't know how to respond.

"I don't blame you. He acted pretty ugly on Saturday." A little more firewood was tossed upon the flames. "But no. He's never done anything more than yell. His tongue hurts us badly enough."

I tried to move a bit more, winced, and finally was able to say, "I'm glad you're okay."

After that tense moment or two, we talked about school. Right then, that was all we had in common. He even asked if Netty was my girlfriend. I told him how we had been friends for so long, but that so far nothing romantic had occurred between us. I left out the part that I would not mind if it had.

A light went on. He had not answered my second question. "How did you get out here alone?"

"Well, it was kind of by accident." He sat up, suddenly energetic. "I knew I wanted to help, so after school I had my mom drop me off at the end of your driveway." He paused to collect his thoughts.

"As I approached I saw a few guys going into the woods, so I just followed. They didn't even know I was behind them." He proceeded to tell me he had been walking quite a while when he heard Artie, crossed his path, and how Artie seemed to be telling Jeremy to follow him.

"He barked. Then he ran away a bit and looked back. Then he barked some more and took a few more steps in the same direction."

"Wait a minute," I interrupted. "Didn't you sign in?"

"Was I supposed to sign in someplace?"

I smacked my forehead. "Duh! What if you became lost while looking for me? Who would know you were even out here?"

He was stunned. It became obvious he had not thought things through. A worried expression grew on his face. I suddenly knew what he was thinking.

"Jake, until my mother puts two and two together, nobody *will* know I'm out here!" It was then that we realized we had put all our eggs in a basket named "Artie".

CHAPTER 45

It was just after dawn that we were discovered. Netty's dad was part of the group who found us. They were impressed that we had been able to start a campfire and maintain it, and I felt lucky since no one asked where we found materials dry enough to burn. I dodged a bullet there.

The med techs checked both of us before they would let anyone move us. Something the younger EMT shot into my leg greatly reduced my pain. Standing behind them, Mr. Carter watched us be prepped while he spoke to us.

"The two of you really stirred the pot," he said. "If I was the dad for either of you, I'm not sure if I'd hug you first or ground you for a year."

"Not the smartest thing I've done," I admitted. Then in an instant, I realized I'd forgotten to say the words that absolutely had to be said.

"Mr. Carter," I asked weakly as I forced myself into my best acting performance. "Has anyone found Gramma?" To not ask that question would have seemed selfish, for that's what started the entire escapade. She *was* the real reason all of us were in the forest in the first place.

After he answered me I felt my head begin to spin. I remember feeling Jeremy patting me on my shoulder, and I saw what I thought was a bizarre smile on Mr. Carter's face. It might have been a grimace. Other than that, I do not remember much of what happened to me for the next several hours, let alone the amount of time I was later told they took to extract me from the woods. That which I recall after my return to our house or my trip to the E R is fragmented at best.

Jeremy asked permission to help carry me once they passed my stretcher over the stone wall along our property. I remember hearing *that*. For a time, there were several voices that blended. Mom's was first.

"Oh my gosh! My gosh!" she shrieked. "Is he going to be okay? Jake, are you—"

Next I heard Mr. Carter. "Danielle, he's a lucky young—"

"Somebody back the ambulance up!"

Voice after voice floated around me. One after another people were speaking, and not many of them were making sense. I was so confused, and I just could not bring myself to speak. I heard one of the E.M.T.'s emphasize to Mom that my injury was not life-threatening, but he was sure I was suffering a degree of shock. Oddly, that was the part I understood.

Just then my dad joined my mother's side. By now I was on a gurney, and the techs gave them a moment to speak to me. Only then was I beginning to comprehend parts of conversation around me.

"Jake, it's me...Dad." He was obviously uncertain about how much I was understanding. "Jake."

I looked at my mother and squeezed her cold hand. "Hi, Mom." Then I tilted my head at my father. "Hi, Dad. I'm sorry–"

"Just rest, Son. Things will be fine."

They asked whether or not one of them could ride along with me in the ambulance. Permission was granted.

By then, I sensed there were a ton of folks gathered around. Perhaps they were volunteers from Search and Rescue. His voice familiar, I did hear Mr. Carter one more time. Everyone must have heard him.

"Dan, I don't know who *this* young man is," he said loudly to my dad as he pointed to Teller, "but he's quite a hero. Just after dark, he was first to find Jake. Somehow he stabilized him. He knew enough to elevate Jake's leg and even built a fire. At some point, he covered Jake with his own sweatshirts, and he kept him awake. This young man wouldn't leave Jake's side this morning either, turning down the chance to get back home sooner and be warm."

A bit on edge, the round of applause and whistling meant to acknowledge Jeremy's efforts made me jumpy. It was thunderous. Two sounds which followed the applause for Jeremy had a soothing effect. Artie started barking which meant he had made it back home safely. I could hear people laughing as he howled, too.

Then as I was about to be placed in the ambulance I had a moment of even greater clarity. I heard Netty calling my name, and from the sound of her voice she was getting closer fast.

"Jake!" she puffed out breathlessly after her sprint. "Mom says you're gonna be okay!" Then right in front of everyone, she leaned down and kissed me!

The last words I understood before the ambulance ride were those of my newest friend Jeremy Teller. With a big grin he whispered to me, "I thought she wasn't your girlfriend, Jake."

Albeit drug induced, I *was* able to utter three words: "Shut up, Teller."

The ambulance ride was a blur. I know Mom was along with me, but I was once again in some sort of mental stupor. The frustrating part was that I was aware of my mental state. I knew I was responding to questions stupidly, and I knew I appeared incoherent. Alert but not alert. Aware but unable to respond. Was this the effect of some painkiller? There were spells when my thoughts were trapped inside my body. One minute I was lucid and could express myself, and at others I could not.

"I hurt my leg, not my head," I said to myself. "What is going on?"

Once in the Emergency Room my wound received the necessary care. I felt nothing. I understood a little. Occasionally I overheard the word "shock" and began to accept it was indeed the source of my problem. A clear thought I do recall was when I heard a familiar female voice explain to my parents how an injury, great or small, can shock an individual. I heard the same voice say that surgery was necessary. Barely able to open my eyes, I struggled to do so. There stood Donna Kammer, long time family friend and ER nurse.

"Any debris inside Jake's leg must be removed and the penetrated area needs to be irrigated to fight off the possibility of infection." She saw my eyes and ran her fingers atop my head. It felt good to know she was in charge.

My dad asked, "Were any bones broken?"

Donna whispered as she stood by my side, "Miraculously no bones were broken, nor did the stick rupture or even scrape any blood vessels."

"What is the long range prognosis for an injury like this?" Mom asked her. "Will he walk, run, and things like that?"

"He'll need antibiotic therapy as well as physical therapy, but he's young." She started to push me down a hall. "The doctors will tell you more."

Lights and ceiling tiles passed overhead in cadence as I was wheeled to a room on a padded gurney. I was being kept at least overnight for observation. An elevator ride became part of the tour, and I recall thinking how things were pretty crowded.

I wanted to ask, "Why am I feeling like this?" I was frustrated and confused. I wanted to scream, "Why I am I like this?" Just as quickly, however, I passed it off as shock since that is what I heard over and over.

Well if my rescue was a shock, my next experience can best be labeled as an explosion! I was lifted to my bed, a drip IV bag was secured above me, and a nurse pulled back my curtain and blew me away. Immediately I knew what triggered my confused mental state back in the forest. Between my parents in the chair right next to my bed sat my grandmother!

As I looked from my pillow at her smile, I let my mind drift back to the woods. I could hear my talk with Mr. Carter all over again.

"The two of you really stirred the pot," he said. "If I was the dad for either of you, I'm not sure if I'd hug you first or ground you for a year."

"Not the smartest thing I've done," I admitted. Then in an instant, I realized I'd forgotten to say the words that absolutely had to be said.

"Mr. Carter," I asked weakly as I forced myself into my best acting performance. "Has anyone found Gramma?"

Mr. Carter smiled and said, "She's fine, Jake. We found her last night long before we found the two of you. She's going to be fine."

It had been Mr. Carter's news that triggered my surprise and subsequent shock. I had just seen my grandmother disappear yesterday with my grandfather while standing with him under a dome of light. For her to be "fine" was beyond my comprehension. First the dome of light and now this? My brain did not know what to believe. How much of what I had just been through was the truth?

The spinning nearly began again. Was I hallucinating? Could this have been a side affect? Was it true that she was sitting there?

"Gramma?" I stammered. "Is it really you?"

She smiled at me and said, "Try to rest, Jacob. You've had quite an experience." Her hand was on my arm, and her touch was real. Imagine that.

"An 'experience'," I thought. "My mysterious grandmother just called it an 'experience'."

"What about—"

"Shhhhhh," she insisted. "We'll talk more later." She looked deep into my eyes. I sensed there was a hint of telepathy in the air. "When we are alone, I will explain everything" is what she was really saying. "You need not worry about the rings, the gold necklace or the letter."

My parents agreed I needed rest. Dad said he would stay with me through the night to keep me company.

He kissed Mom on her cheek and said kindly, "Danielle, you two can go home. Make some calls, and then get some rest." He ran his fingers gently across the top of my head. "We will see you both in the morning."

EPILOGUE

At the last moment, Gramma decided she was just not ready. Being the wonderful husband that he is, Grampa understood, just as she understood his need to go on ahead. And, being the great salesman he is, Grampa convinced his *boss* that the best place for Gramma was back with us. In a nutshell, that is what went down.

WNEP's James Hamill had an amazing story to tell. Search crews set out to rescue one person, and they ended up saving three! Of the three, one young man, Jeremy Teller, was hailed a hero. Not only was he thanked in his own town, but also around the country since WNEP's parent station labeled him "Person of the Week" by Friday night on the ABC Nightly News with David Muir!

Jeremy's grandfather and Crown Developers did not fare as well. Largely due to his own ignorant outburst after what had been a successful roadside cleanup project, enough witnesses spread the word regarding the now ex-Commissioner's behavior. His November bid for reelection was tantamount to the success of President Nixon's Watergate.

For Jake, things returned close to normal considering his circumstances. In middle school terms, Netty and Jake were a "couple" and their mothers could not have been happier.

Not long after Jake's recovery had begun, one evening there was a brief report on NBC's Inside Edition, the popular television show hosted by two-time Emmy Winner Deborah Norville. Only twenty seconds in length, her feature expressed curiosity regarding recent rumors concerning the growing number of unexplainable appearances and disappearances of old stone bridges around the world. The McGees might have heard her report if they were not in their kitchen with the Carters enjoying Netty's chocolate birthday cake with peanut butter frosting.

IN CASE YOU DIDN'T KNOW...

Will Wyckoff's first novel, **Birds on a Wire**, was published in 2012.

A non-political story about the power of family, friendship, and redemption, it recounts the efforts of fictional U.S. President Elijah Rittenhouse as he attempts to prevent the murder of his friend Eli Parks at the hands of a beautiful North Korean assassin, Hyun Lee.

Birds on a Wire is available in the following manner:

1) Via Createspace e-store: www.createspace.com/3727575
2) Amazon.com books (Please check out its Amazon reviews!)
3) Kindle

Or

4) Contact Will Wyckoff to order a **personalized, autographed** copy via Facebook or his email address: upstairs@ptd.net

Feel free to provide reader feedback as well!

70253994R00151

Made in the USA
Columbia, SC
02 May 2017